Her photog
justice.

Not by a long shot.

Even though Royce was watching her from half a room away, Shara Atwood was so alive she lit up the room. It wasn't just the sinuous way she was dancing—which he had to admit was incredibly hot—she seemed to radiate a vibrant kind of energy that made it impossible not to look at her.

And people *were* looking—in their droves.

Royce was watching Shara because he *had* to.

Because as of an hour ago it was his *job* to watch her.

What irritated him was the fact that he was enjoying it. The prickling sensation under his skin told him that his body was enjoying it even more—a fact that he found doubly infuriating.

Tina Duncan lives in trendy inner-city Sydney, with her partner Edy. With a background in marketing and event management, she now spends her days running a business with Edy. She's a multi-tasking expert. When she's not busy typing up quotes and processing invoices, she's writing. She loves being physically active, and enjoys tennis (both watching and playing), bushwalking and dancing. Spending quality time with her family and friends also rates high on her priority list. She has a weakness for good food and fine wine, and has a sweet tooth she has to keep under control.

Recent titles by the same author:

HER SECRET, HIS LOVE-CHILD
DA SILVA'S MISTRESS

**Did you know these are also available as eBooks?
Visit www.millsandboon.co.uk**

PLAYING HIS DANGEROUS GAME

BY
TINA DUNCAN

First published in Great Britain 2011
by Mills & Boon, an imprint of Harlequin (UK) Limited.
Harlequin (UK) Limited, Eton House, 18-24 Paradise Road,
Richmond, Surrey TW9 1SR

© Tina Duncan 2011

ISBN: 978 0 263 88716 7

Harlequin (UK) policy is to use papers that are natural, renewable and recyclable products and made from wood grown in sustainable forests. The logging and manufacturing process conform to the legal environmental regulations of the country of origin.

Printed and bound in Spain
by Blackprint CPI, Barcelona

PLAYING HIS
DANGEROUS
GAME

CHAPTER ONE

HER photograph didn't do her justice.

Not by a long shot.

Even though Royce was watching her from half a room away, Shara Atwood was so alive she lit up the room. It wasn't just the sinuous way she was dancing—which he had to admit was incredibly hot—but she seemed to radiate a vibrant kind of energy that made it impossible not to look at her.

And people *were* looking—in their droves.

The young single men at the club were outright staring. The older men, or those accompanied by their wives or girl-friends, were not so obvious. Their eyes slid to Shara whenever they thought they could get away with it without being caught.

Royce fitted neither of those categories.

He was watching Shara because he *had* to.

Because as of an hour ago it was his *job* to watch her.

What irritated him was the fact that he was enjoying it. The prickling sensation under his skin told him that his body was enjoying it even more—a fact that he found doubly ir-ritating.

Shara Atwood was the type of woman Royce despised.

She might be beautiful and sexy, but by all accounts she was also spoilt, selfish and self-centred.

He knew the type and tried to steer clear of them—except when his job made that task impossible.

The reminder of why he was here prompted Royce to straighten away from the wall. He made his way through the crowd towards the dance floor. Everyone moved automatically out of his way. At six-foot-four and being keenly muscled, he had that effect on people. They no doubt thought it was safer to move than to accidentally collide with him.

He stopped on the edge of the dance floor.

Now that he was closer Royce realised that Shara had her eyes closed. She was swaying and twirling in perfect time to the music and ignoring everything and everyone around her—including the eager young man with the light brown hair who was desperately trying to capture her attention.

As he watched, the young man reached out to take hold of her shoulders, but she shook him off without even bothering to look at him, as if he were no more important than a bothersome fly. The young man said something. Royce was too far away to hear what it was, but not too far to read Shara's expression.

A flash of irritation she made no effort to hide crossed her face and then her full lips parted. Whatever she'd said, it must have been cutting. The young man jumped back as if he'd been stung by a wasp. His cheeks flushed a bright fiery red as he turned and stalked off the dance floor.

'Keep on walking, mate,' Royce muttered under his breath. 'And don't look back. She's not worth it.'

The incident was a timely reminder to focus on business rather than on Shara's lusciously full figure and thick fall of sable hair.

He walked across the dance floor and stopped right in front of her.

Then he said her name.

Shara kept right on dancing as if she hadn't heard him.

But she had.

Royce *knew* she had.

To the casual observer her expression hadn't changed, but Royce was an expert at reading body language. He was trained to scrutinise people and assess their reactions. That kind of attention to detail was essential in his line of work.

He'd captured the imperceptible tightening of her mouth and the barely there contraction of her brow. And even though her movements were still fluid and graceful there had been a momentary stiffness—so brief it had almost been invisible—that had run through her curvaceous frame.

It was clear she was irritated by the interruption.

Well, she could be irritated all she liked.

Royce was not like the young pup she'd just sent away with his tail between his legs.

He was a man.

And he didn't like being ignored—particularly when he had a job to do.

'Shara,' he said again.

That was all he said. Nothing else.

But his tone, which fell somewhere between firm and harsh, was one people usually ignored at their peril.

Shara heaved a sigh.

Why couldn't everyone leave her alone?

OK. So she'd made a mistake coming to the club tonight. She knew that. Had known it since the minute she'd walked through the door.

She wasn't in the mood to party. She hadn't been for a long time. The last twelve months had seen to that.

She'd also outgrown the crowd she'd used to run with—a fact she'd realised within minutes of arriving at the club. She could thank the last twelve months for that too.

She had to face it. Coming here tonight was just another poor decision in a long, *long* line of poor decisions. Stuffing up appeared to be a habit she just couldn't break.

'Shara.'

There it was again. That voice. She didn't recognise it. She would have remembered if she'd heard it before.

It was male. Very definitely male. A deep baritone that made her toes curl in the stiletto sandals she was wearing.

Not Tony, thank goodness. How many times did she have to tell the guy she wasn't interested? The way he kept coming on to her was bordering on harassment, and with one man already making a nuisance out of himself she didn't need another.

Perhaps that was why tonight she'd given up on politely rejecting Tony's overtures and given it to him straight.

Tony had been gone for no more than five seconds before this guy with the deep velvety voice had appeared.

If she ignored him maybe he'd take the hint and go away.

'Shara.'

No such luck. There it was again, only harder this time. Like a hammer hitting concrete.

Whoever he was, he wasn't going away in a hurry. That tone spoke of stubbornness and determination—qualities that none of the people in this crowd possessed.

Curious in spite of herself, Shara stopped moving and opened her eyes.

She found herself staring at the middle of a strong, barrel-like chest.

She looked up. And up.

Whoever he was, he was tall.

He was also lip-smackingly gorgeous.

Not that he was handsome in the traditional sense—his face was too hard, too angular. But he was ruggedly good-looking, with a broad forehead, strong, well-defined jaw and a slightly crooked nose that somehow did nothing to detract from his tough handsomeness.

He was perfectly proportioned too. Strongly muscled thighs and a stomach that was flat and hard balanced his broad shoulders and deep chest. And he was so big. Even his hands, which he was holding loosely at his sides, were large.

Would his—?

A hot flush of colour flooded her cheeks. Even though she'd managed to put a brake on her thoughts, she couldn't stop her eyes dropping and felt the breath catch in her throat. He was built in proportion, all right…

A peculiar weakness invaded her knees. What on earth had got into her? Imagine staring at him like that! She'd never done anything like that before. And then an appalling thought occurred to her. God, what if he'd noticed…?

Her eyes snapped to his face.

His total lack of expression meant she couldn't tell one way or another.

Embarrassed by the way she'd stared at his private parts, and annoyed by the weakness invading her knees, she snapped, 'What, damn it?'

Royce stared into the most amazing blue eyes he'd ever seen. They were bluer than the sky on a bright summer's day, brighter than a freshly cut sapphire, and more mysterious than the depths of the ocean.

It would be easy to be captivated by them but Royce was not easily captivated—particularly when her sharp, stinging voice told him the true measure of the woman standing in front of him.

'So you *are* polite enough to look at someone when they're speaking to you, are you?' Royce asked, returning sting for sting with rapier-sharp speed.

Her magnificent eyes narrowed and her chin lifted fractionally into the air. 'Do I know you?'

It was a simple question, but the way she asked it was anything but simple.

Princess talk.

That was the way Royce labelled her tone.

These society babes had a way of talking down to someone when they wanted to. Her tone implied that she couldn't possibly know someone like *him*.

A lesser man might have been embarrassed, or even have walked away. But Royce was made of tougher stuff than that. So he smiled and said, 'No, but we're about to become acquainted.'

Her eyes narrowed some more, then her mouth moved in a disparaging little twist, and somehow, despite being about a foot shorter than he was, she managed to look down the length of her nose at him. 'I don't think so. You're not my type.'

'Don't worry, lady. You're not my type either,' Royce drawled smoothly, not the least put out by her attempted insult. 'I'm here in a purely professional capacity.'

Her expression shifted, lost its regal look. She ran her eyes over him again. She'd done that before, when she'd first opened her eyes. Royce had been disconcerted by his response to that simple look, his blood vessels expanding and heat flowing under his skin.

The same thing was happening again now, and he liked it even less the second time around.

'Well, if you're the bouncer I hate to tell you this but I've done nothing wrong. I'm just minding my own business and dancing. So why don't you go away?' She made a waving movement through the air with her hand. 'Go on. Shoo.'

Royce almost laughed. What she'd said, combined with the action, was just so ridiculous. As if he were a pesky animal she was trying to get rid of.

'I'm not a bouncer. Your father asked me to bring you home.'

Her expression became instantly wary. 'He did?'

Royce nodded. 'Yes. Are you ready to leave?'

Shara shook her head, sending her thick pelt of dark hair swirling around her shoulders.

Royce tried to suppress his irritation. He didn't like doing this kind of job. These days he usually restricted himself to overseeing the business. If he did get involved he chose investigative or security cases, *not* bodyguarding. He allocated those jobs to somebody else.

But this was different. Gerard Atwood, head of Atwood Industries, was one of his best clients—if not *the* best. When Gerard had said protecting his daughter would be a personal favour to him Royce had known he couldn't refuse. Not unless he wanted to lose one of his biggest clients—which he didn't.

'Well, if you need to collect your bag and say your goodbyes make it quick. I want to get out of here.'

Although this was a reputable club that didn't mean Shara was safe. After all, it had taken less than twenty minutes of research for *him* to locate her, so no doubt her ex-husband could do the same.

Even before he'd finished speaking Shara was shaking her head. 'That wasn't what I meant.'

His eyes narrowed. 'Then what did you mean?'

She folded her arms. It drew his attention—*unwilling* attention—to the thrusting swell of her breasts.

She was what his mother would call generously endowed. Somehow Royce knew her breasts would fill his hands perfectly—which was no mean feat, given that his hands were on the large size.

The thought sent a prickle of desire along his nerve-endings.

'I'm not going anywhere with you,' Shara said, looking at him down the length of her nose again.

Her tone stopped the prickle dead in its tracks. 'Yes, you are.'

'No, I am not.'

Royce sighed. 'Why not?'

'I have no idea who you are. I only have your word for it that my father sent you.'

'Good point.' In fact it was a very good point. He hadn't introduced himself. He hadn't explained the situation. He'd been sufficiently distracted by the sinuous sway of her body and then annoyed by the way she'd treated first the young guy and then himself that he'd not only put the niceties aside but also his professionalism.

He should know better than that.

'I'm from the Royce Agency. Have you heard of them?'

She nodded. 'Yes. I have. My father uses them all the time. If I'm to believe their spiel they are the largest and most well-known security firm on the globe.'

'It's not spiel. We are the biggest and the best,' Royce said proudly.

It would be fourteen years next month since he'd started the Royce Agency. He'd only been twenty at the time, operating out of the spare bedroom in his parents' home in northern Sydney. It had taken hard work and long hours to make it what it was today.

Shara shrugged. 'Whatever.'

Royce refused to be insulted. As he'd learned a long time ago, these society babes didn't care about anything or anyone except themselves.

Reaching into his back pocket, he pulled out a brown leather wallet. Flipping it open, he held it out to her.

Her arms remained folded in front of her. 'What's that?'

'My driver's licence. I thought you might want to see some identification.'

She shook her head. 'That's not necessary.'

Royce frowned. 'It's entirely necessary. You can't just walk out of here with a perfect stranger. You can't trust anybody these days. You have to be cautious.'

'Again, you misunderstand me. It's not necessary because I have no intention of leaving with you.'

The silence that followed her words was filled with the sound of music and chatter. Royce ignored it all. So did Shara.

He thrust his wallet closer. 'Take it. Look at it. Because you *will* be leaving with me.'

She sighed and snatched the wallet from his hand.

Shara's head bowed as she examined his licence intently. Royce stared at the luxurious fall of raven-black hair that fell about her shoulders and resisted the urge to reach out and stroke it.

'Royce as in *the* Royce?' she asked, looking up from his wallet and giving him a suspicious look.

'At your service,' Royce acknowledged, holding out his hand.

She eyed his hand as if it was a snake he was extending to her, then with obvious reluctance placed her hand in his.

They both felt what happened next.

Royce just wasn't sure how to explain it.

It reminded him of the zap of static electricity that built up on your shoes on a windy day that zapped your hand the minute you touched something metallic.

Only it wasn't that.

It also reminded him of the pins and needles you got when you accidentally fell asleep on your arm.

Only it wasn't quite like that either.

It was just a…

Well, it was just a sensation—like an energy transfer of some kind.

No doubt there would be a scientific explanation for it if he bothered looking for one.

Shara snatched her hand out of his, her wide eyes fixed on his face. 'So. You…you own the Royce Agency?' she asked, showing the first crack in her composure since they'd met.

'I'm afraid so.'

'Well, Mr Royce, I—'

Royce shook his head. 'It's not Mr Royce. It's just plain Royce.'

Shara looked back down at the driver's licence she still held. 'It says A. Royce right here.' She held up the wallet and pointed with a red-varnished nail to the small print. 'That makes you Mr Royce.'

Royce brushed aside the lock of hair that had fallen across his forehead. 'Technically, I suppose it does. But as far as I'm concerned my father is Mr Royce. Everyone just calls me Royce.'

'Why don't they call you by your first name?'

'Because I don't like my first name,' he explained calmly.

'Why? What is it?'

'That's none of your business.'

'I don't suppose it is.'

Royce felt as if they'd got way off track. 'Well, are you satisfied that I am who I say I am?'

She nodded. 'I am, but I'm still not going with you.'

Royce held on to his temper with difficulty. The fact that she'd rather stay here partying with this shallow crowd instead of honouring her father's request told him a lot about her.

Lack of respect. Selfishness.

He could go on, but what was the point?

It wouldn't get the job done, and the job was the only thing that mattered.

'Please will you reconsider?' he said persuasively. 'Your father was most insistent.'

For a moment she looked undecided, then she waved a hand. 'All right. Lead the way Just Plain Royce. We can't keep my father waiting, now, can we?'

The journey to Atwood Hall was completed in silence.

Royce tried to make polite conversation several times,

but Shara's monosyllabic answers eventually forced him to give up.

When they reached the two-storey sandstone house Shara headed straight for her father's study. She pushed the door open without knocking.

Royce followed her in.

She stopped in the middle of the room then swung around to face him. 'Where is he?'

Royce folded his arms. 'On a plane to New York.'

Her mouth dropped open. 'Then what was all that crap about my father wanting to see me?'

He stared back at her calmly. 'I never said anything about your father wanting to see you. All I said was that he asked me to bring you home. Which he did…' He paused for a heart-beat. 'About thirty minutes before he left for the airport.'

The silence that filled the room prickled at the back of his neck.

Shara's thick lashes dropped down to shield her expression.

Royce didn't feel guilty about the minor deception. Gerard had warned him that Shara was unlikely to co-operate. You had to treat uncooperative 'principals'—which was the industry term for the person you were protecting—in much the same way a lawyer would treat a hostile witness.

With a firm hand and any tactic you could lay your hands on.

If keeping Shara safe meant bending the rules a fraction and allowing her to jump to the wrong conclusion then so be it. He'd do what he had to do—an attitude which had contributed in no small measure to his success.

Finally Shara looked up. 'Why? Why did my father want you to bring me home?'

'He didn't think going to the club was a good idea and I happen to agree with him.'

Her cheeks reddened, although he couldn't tell whether

it was from embarrassment or anger. 'I don't care what you think. What I do, and when I do it, is none of your business.'

'That's where you're wrong. Everything you do from now on is very much my business.'

She frowned. 'What's that supposed to mean?'

'It means that while your father is overseas I will be looking after you.'

Shara blinked, frowned, and blinked again. 'I don't need looking after.'

'No? That's not the way I understand it.'

'Well, I don't care what you understand. I'm a little too old for a babysitter, don't you think?'

'I'm not a babysitter. I'm a bodyguard.'

'Babysitter. Bodyguard.' She waved a hand through the air. Her breasts jiggled. Royce tried not to notice but failed miserably. 'It's all the same to me. Either one is completely unnecessary.'

Although Royce didn't particularly like what he was hearing, he had no objection to Shara speaking her mind. If there was one thing he couldn't stand it was someone saying one thing to his face and then saying—or doing—the exact opposite behind his back.

'Well, your father disagrees,' Royce said calmly.

'I—'

Royce cut her off. 'You're wasting your breath. Gerard warned me that this would be your attitude and he said to tell you that while you're living under his roof you'll follow his rules.'

Her humiliation was complete.

Shara stared at the tips of her red-varnished toenails as if her life depended upon it. Tears pricked at the backs of her eyes but she blinked them away.

She had no intention of bursting into tears. That would only add to her humiliation.

Right now all she wanted to do was curl up into a ball and pretend that the rest of the world didn't exist.

It was a feeling she knew all too well. But she fought against it. If there was one thing the last twelve months had taught her it was not to give in to feelings of helplessness. She had to be strong and stand up for herself.

It didn't matter how many times she got knocked down. She had to pick herself up, brush herself off, and try again.

So she straightened her shoulders, dragged in a breath, and instead of avoiding eye contact lifted her head and deliberately looked Just Plain Royce directly in the eye.

His face was expressionless. She had no idea what he was thinking and frankly she didn't care.

She waved a hand through the air. 'Well, Mr Just Plain Royce, I'm out of here.'

He folded his arms across his impressive chest. 'And where, pray tell, are you planning on going?'

She put her hands on her hips. 'That is none of your business!'

'Correction. As I said, where you go and what you do *is* my business.' His tone was determined. 'My job is to protect you. It will help if I know where you're going at all times.'

Her already straight shoulders straightened some more. 'My father may have hired you, but I have no desire for a bodyguard. You can do what the hell you like, but don't expect any help from me!'

A look that was part resignation, part irritation flashed across his face before his expression hardened. 'Be warned. I intend doing my job, with or without your co-operation. It will be easier on both of us if you work with me, but it's not entirely necessary. If you want to act like a rebellious teenager then go right ahead. I won't stop you.'

Shara would have laughed except it wasn't really funny. She'd been a well-behaved, follow-the-rules, obedient teenager. A real goody-two-shoes, in fact.

Twelve months of marriage to Steve Brady had shown her that being meek and biddable had its drawbacks—big-time!

She'd emerged from the dark tunnel of that period a very different person from the one who'd entered it.

She crossed her arms and raised one eyebrow. 'If you're trying reverse psychology on me then it won't work. I'm a grown adult, able to decide when and where I go without reporting in to somebody else.'

His dark eyes glinted. 'Are you? An adult, that is? If so, then prove it.'

She frowned. 'And how am I supposed to do that?'

'Don't go back to the club.'

Shara raised an eyebrow. 'And what will that prove?'

'It will prove you're adult enough to put your safety ahead of having a good time,' Royce said calmly.

The word 'adult' rankled. She wasn't a child. Her marriage had made her grow up—fast.

She knew what she was doing; she was making a stand.

She was sick and tired of the men in her life—first her father and then her husband—telling her what to do.

She didn't need to add a bossy bodyguard to the list.

If she slunk off to her room with her tail between her legs then wasn't she just handing over her power to Royce?

Well, she'd been there, done that, and she'd suffered because of it.

She could, and she would, make her own decisions.

Mr Just Plain Royce had better start getting used to it.

And why was she calling him that anyway?

Plain was ordinary. Easily overlooked. Royce was neither of those things. In fact just the opposite.

'I don't have to prove anything to you,' she said, clasping her hands together in front of her. 'I'm twenty-three years old. I *am* an adult. And if you think insulting me will force me to co-operate then you're sorely mistaken.'

He held up his hands, a small smile twisting his mouth.

'That accusation is well and truly misdirected, I can assure you. That kind of strategy would never work with you. I know that.'

She raised a brow. 'And how do you know that?'

Royce shrugged. 'Because I've seen you in action. First at the club and then again here.'

She gave him a puzzled frown. 'Meaning?'

'Meaning that using reverse psychology on you would have the reverse effect.' He waved a hand, with a glint in his eyes that made her want to hit him. 'You're determined not to co-operate no matter what. It doesn't matter what I say or do, you're going to do your own thing and to hell with everyone else. If I push all it will do is make you dig your heels in even more.'

Shara gnashed her teeth.

She had a sneaking suspicion that Royce was right—although it would take someone pulling out her fingernails before she'd admit it.

'You haven't got a clue what you're talking about,' she flung at him. At that moment the old grandfather clock in the entrance hall struck the hour. Shara glanced at her watch. 'Well, it looks like you're going to get your way. I'm not going back to the club. Not because you say I shouldn't, but because it's late and I'm tired. Goodnight.'

Without another word she spun on her heel to leave the room, but his next words stopped her. 'Before you go perhaps you'd like to tell me which bedroom is yours.'

Slowly she turned back to face him. Her heart was beating with slow, heavy thumps. 'Why on earth do you want to know that?'

'Because I'll be taking up residence in the room next to yours, of course.'

A hand made its way to the base of her throat, where she could feel the beat of her pulse under her skin. For a moment she'd thought…

Well, she wasn't sure exactly what she'd thought.

But whatever it was it had made her go hot all over.

Her hands slammed down on her hips. 'You most certainly will not!'

Royce gestured to the corner of the room. A large black suitcase she hadn't noticed before was sitting there. 'I most certainly will.'

She shook her head. 'I don't understand.'

'I'll be living here for the duration. I—'

'Living here...? You can't do that!'

'Why not?'

'Well, because you just can't.' Shara blinked rapidly, the blinks timing perfectly with the increased rhythm of her heart.

It was out of the question.

Out of the question for any number of reasons—one of which she didn't want to examine too closely because she suspected it had something to do with the little curl of sensation she experienced low in the pit of her belly every time she looked at him.

'Well, I'm afraid what you want doesn't come into it. As your father is aware, I have a policy of up close and personal at the Royce Agency.'

'What does that mean?' Shara asked suspiciously, her brain leapfrogging into all sorts of thoughts. Just how personal did they get at this agency of his?

'It means I'm guarding *you*, not your house.' He shrugged his broad shoulders. 'I'll be of absolutely no use to you if I'm sitting outside in my car and your ex-husband breaks in through the back door, will I?'

'I guess not.' The suggestion was enough to send a shiver of fear slicing down her spine. It was something that hadn't occurred to her. The very idea of Steve breaking in filled her with dread. She swallowed, clasping her hands tightly together in front of her. 'I just expected—'

'That it would be just like on TV?' he finished resignedly, sounding as though he'd heard it all a million times before. 'Well, it's not. You either show me where you sleep or I'll find out for myself. Either way, I'm staying. And I'm staying where I can keep an eye on you.'

'Have it your own way,' Shara muttered.

If Royce intended to hang around there wasn't much she could do about it. He was too big for her to throw out. And there was no use complaining to the police because he had her father's permission to be here—something that one phone call would establish.

All she could do was call her father in the morning and see if she could change his mind.

If she couldn't she'd just have to put up with the situation as best she could. She'd put up with a hell of a lot worse.

This was no big deal.

All she had to do was ignore Royce.

Just go about her business as if he wasn't there.

Except she had the uneasy feeling Royce wasn't going to be easy to ignore.

'I certainly shall,' Royce said.

He spoke with the kind of confidence Shara envied. That I'm-sure-of-my-place-in-the-world kind of confidence. The kind that made every decision he made rock-solid and unbreakable. He knew exactly where he was going—and how to get there.

By contrast, Shara didn't have a clue where she was going.

Even though she was only twenty-three, she'd taken so many wrong turns in her life it was ridiculous. She felt like a player in a Snakes and Ladders game who always landed on the snake's head and slid back down to the tail.

She felt as if that had just happened again.

Her attempt to stand up for herself and control her own destiny had just been ripped out from underneath her and she'd landed flat on her face—again.

'You'd better follow me,' she said through gritted teeth.

She spun on her heel and stalked from the room.

Royce picked up his suitcase and followed her.

'This is my room,' Shara said, indicating a door with a wave of her hand. 'You can sleep next door. The room is made up. I'll just check that you have some towels.'

'Thank you.'

She inclined her head and went inside. Assured that he had everything he needed, she walked to the door, pausing just inside the doorway. 'Goodnight.'

'Goodnight, Shara.'

The way he said her name made her toes curl in her sandals. She hurried from the room.

An hour later she lay, staring up at the ceiling.

For weeks, if not months, her last thought before going to sleep had been about Steve and the hell he'd put her through—was still putting her through.

But tonight was different.

For the first time in a long time she wasn't thinking about her ex-husband.

Another man had super-imposed himself in her mind's eye.

A large man called Just Plain Royce.

CHAPTER TWO

THE next morning Shara followed the smell of cooking bacon to the kitchen.

Since their housekeeper only came in on weekdays, and didn't help herself to breakfast when she was there, Shara knew exactly who was cooking.

Just Plain Royce.

She was tempted to go back to her room and wait until he'd finished, but that smacked a little too strongly of running away so she squared her shoulders determinedly and walked in.

Royce was standing at the stove, his back to the door. He was wearing well-washed denim jeans and a tight white T-shirt, both of which hugged his muscle-packed body.

Of their own volition her eyes made a sweeping perusal—from his still wet hair, down the strong planes of his back, to his backside and legs.

Her heart kerthumped—then did it again.

He really was a fine figure of a man. Although the fact that she kept on noticing annoyed the hell out of her.

'You've made yourself at home,' she said sarcastically.

He half turned towards her, one thick dark eyebrow raised. 'I hope you don't expect me to live here and not eat?'

She shrugged. 'I'd prefer it if you weren't living here at

all, but we've already had that argument so there's no point having it again, is there?'

'I suppose not.' He paused for a moment and then asked, 'Did you call your father?'

'Yes. You must have known I would.'

'I did. And what did he say?'

Her father had said a lot. About how he was concerned about her. About how he knew what was best for her.

Etc. Etc. Etc.

He had no idea how much she'd changed from the girl who used to live with him. And she couldn't tell him without revealing things she didn't want him to know.

He knew her marriage had been bad, but he had no idea how bad.

'You're still here, aren't you?' she said by way of answer.

'I guess I am,' he said neutrally, turning back to the stove.

Shara eyed the frying pan and the small mountain of chopped items on the cutting board waiting to be cooked. 'When is the army arriving?'

Royce shrugged his broad shoulders. His muscles rippled under his T-shirt, doing strange things to Shara's tummy muscles. 'I'm a big man. I need lots of food. And since I work out regularly it's important to keep up my intake of protein and carbohydrates.' He waved a spatula through the air. 'Do you want some?'

Shara shuddered and made her way to the fridge. 'No. Unlike you, I have a small appetite. Fruit and yoghurt suits me just fine.'

He made a sound that was indecipherable.

Shara turned away from the fridge with a punnet of strawberries in one hand and a tub of yoghurt in the other. 'What does *ugh* mean?'

'Nothing. I just don't approve of women who think they can live on the smell of an oily rag and just pick at their food. The human body needs good nutrition to be at its best.'

Shara dumped her items on the granite benchtop with more force than was necessary. 'You're jumping to conclusions. Do I *look* like the kind of woman who just picks at her food?'

As soon as the words left her mouth Shara regretted them.

Royce turned to face her. His chocolate brown eyes travelled from the crown of her head to the tips of her toes.

He missed nothing in between. Not a single thing.

Shara knew he didn't because she felt that look as if it were a caress.

Her skin stretched tight in every place his eyes touched. Her nerve-endings prickled. Even her nipples tightened in the confines of her bra.

The sensation in her tummy flickered to life again. Only this time it was like the flame on the stove. A solid burn that made her want to press her hand against her stomach.

Finally their gazes reconnected.

Something flared deep in his eyes—something that made her tremble with reaction.

'No, you don't look like a woman on a constant diet.' Was it her imagination or was the timbre of his voice lower than it had been moments before? 'I approve.'

Her heart thumped.

What did that mean?

I approve.

Approved of what?

The fact that she didn't diet?

Or did he approve of her body?

The fact that it might be the latter made a rush of hot blood hurtle through her system.

She wanted to look away, but her eyes just wouldn't obey. They remained locked on Royce as if they were glued there.

Royce didn't look away either.

The air between them began to pulse, as if a soundless drum were beating.

It wasn't until she saw the thick plume of dark smoke rising up behind him that she broke out of her trance-like state. 'Royce! The pan!'

Royce cursed and spun on his heel. With swift efficiency he turned off the gas, swiped a dishcloth from the bench and flapped it in the air to dissipate the smoke.

Bending down, he inspected the contents of the frying pan.

Straightening, he threw her a mind-numbing smile over his shoulder. 'It's a good job I like my bacon crispy,' he said, picking up a spatula and scooping the bacon on to a plate.

Shara eyed the results. 'That's not crispy. That's dead.'

Royce shrugged. 'Each to their own. I happen to like it that way.'

'Are you sure you're not just saying that because you've burnt it? It takes a man to admit when he's wrong.'

His eyes glinted. 'No, I'm not fibbing. This really is the way I like it.'

Shara grimaced. 'I suppose you like your fried eggs with a runny yolk too?'

He flashed her a grin that made her go weak at the knees. 'You bet. Is there any other way to have them?'

Shara smiled back. Then, realising what she was doing, she forced her mouth into a straight line.

This man was not her friend. He wasn't exactly her enemy either. But he *was* standing between her and something she wanted—which was the right to make her own decisions. That right was something most people took for granted. It wasn't until it was taken away from you that you realised how much you valued it.

'I like mine cooked through,' she muttered, and turned away.

Grabbing a chopping board, she began cutting strawberries with all the attention a surgeon would give to the most complicated and delicate operation.

They worked silently for a while. Much as she tried, Shara couldn't stop her eyes from straying back to him.

For such a big man Royce moved with silent gracefulness, each movement precise and self-assured. Somehow she knew he'd make love the same way.

She flushed, dropping her lashes. She didn't know where the thought had come from but she wished it would go back there.

His competency as a lover was of no interest to her.

Why should it be?

She was over men.

Shara took a seat at the breakfast table and began eating. Royce joined her a few minutes later with a plate piled high with food.

'So, tell me about this ex of yours,' he suggested softly, when he'd demolished half of the plate with considerable gusto.

The mention of her ex-husband almost made her choke on a strawberry. 'He's not my favourite topic of conversation.'

'Perhaps not.' He took a bite of mushroom. 'But the more I know about him the easier it will be for me to do my job.'

Shara angled her chin into the air. 'I don't care. I don't want to talk about him. Besides, I've already told you that I don't want a bodyguard, so why would I want to make your job easier for you?'

She had no intention of answering personal questions.

Painful questions.

And she had no intention of helping him. She didn't want him around, poking his nose in her business. It would be safer—for all of them—if he quit and left her alone.

His expression remained unchanged but his eyes had hardened. 'Maybe because it's the polite thing to do? Maybe because it would give two strangers sharing breakfast something to talk about?'

Shara stared at him over the top of her spoon. 'Actually, I think it's impolite to ask someone you've just met personal and intrusive questions. If you feel we must talk then I can think of at least a dozen more interesting topics than my ex-husband. What about the weather? Or the exorbitant price of petrol—which in my opinion has gotten way out of control?'

Royce snapped off the blackened end of a rasher of bacon, popped it in his mouth and chewed. When he'd swallowed, he said, 'I'd much rather talk about Steve Brady.'

Shara put her spoon down on the table less than gently. 'And I wouldn't. Now, unless you want to talk about something else, I'm leaving.'

Royce sighed. 'Stubborn.'

'Yes.'

And she wasn't about to apologise for it.

She had to protect herself.

No matter what it took.

Royce sighed again—even more heavily. 'Will you at least tell me about how Brady is harassing you?'

Shara sat back against her seat. 'Didn't my father tell you?'

'He mentioned a few phone calls and the fact that the guy has been seen hanging around outside the house.'

Shara stared back steadily, keeping her expression neutral. 'Well, there's nothing more to tell. Dad has summed it up nicely. Which is why hiring you is a complete and utter over-reaction.'

She'd tried telling her father that but he hadn't listened. Maybe he sensed that things were worse than what she'd told him.

'I've known Gerard for a number of years,' Royce said. 'He's not the type to over-react.'

Her chin angled into the air. 'Well, in this case he has.'

Royce stared back at her. 'I'll be the judge of that.'

Royce received ample evidence of Steve Brady's harassment several hours later. He walked into the lounge room, where Shara was sitting flipping through a magazine, just as the phone rang.

He noticed the way she jumped like a scalded cat, and watched as the colour drained out of her face.

'Leave it,' Royce ordered as Shara reached a hand towards the phone.

'Leave it?' Shara asked. 'Why?'

'You think it's him, don't you?' Royce asked. 'Your ex?'

A frown creased the smooth skin of her forehead as she nodded her head slowly.

'Let it ring,' he dismissed.

'Why?'

Royce sank down on the lounger opposite and stretched his legs out in front of him. 'Because I said so.'

Her chin jutted. 'That's not good enough. I'm not a puppy dog. You can't order me to sit, beg or roll over any time you feel like it. If you want me to do something I suggest you remember two things.'

He lifted a brow, trying to ignore how damned sexy she looked. 'And what would those be?'

Her chin lifted even higher. She uncrossed her legs and then recrossed them the other way. The action pulled the fabric of her Capri pants tight around her hips. Royce tried not to stare.

'There's this movie I saw once. It's about a guy whose life is going nowhere until he signs up for a self-help programme based on one simple covenant, which is to say yes to anything and everything. It begins to transform his life.'

'Well, that sounds very interesting, but what has that got to do with you co-operating with me?'

Her eyes—they really were the most magnificent colour—seared into his. 'I've spent a year of my life with a man who has told me what to do and what not to do every minute of every day. When I walked out I made a vow not to let that happen again. So if you want me to do something I suggest you try *asking* me instead of *telling* me.'

'Fine. Please don't answer the phone.' He raised the other brow this time. 'There. Is that better?'

'Yes. Much better,' she said. 'The second thing you need to remember is that I'm not going to do anything unless I know *why*. If you don't want me to answer the phone the least you can do is give me a reason.'

Royce stared at her. He couldn't argue with her approach. He was a logical, facts-and-figures kind of guy. If he were in her situation he'd react the same way.

What he *did* object to was the hoity-toity princess tone of voice she was using. As if she was a queen instructing one of her minions.

Normally her attitude would be water off a duck's back. He'd accepted a long time ago that the rich liked to think they were better than everyone else.

He'd never understood the mindset that the measure of a man lay in how much money he had in his bank account or how large his investment portfolio was.

He hadn't understood it when students at the exclusive boarding school he'd attended had made it clear that a scholarship didn't mean that he belonged. All it meant was that some rich person had bequeathed upon him a privilege he wasn't otherwise entitled to.

He understood the attitude even less now that he was a grown man. A *successful* man. For some reason he'd assumed that his achievements would earn him an automatic entrée into the exclusive club of the wealthy.

Not so.

It also seemed to matter where—or was it how?—you made your money. Inherited wealth made you part of the group; earning it yourself didn't.

In Royce's mind the exact opposite was true. Succeeding off your own bat held a hell of a lot more weight in his view than leeching off someone else's success. Just as the measure of a man should be in how he acted and what he stood for rather than some meaningless dollar value.

Royce was no longer interested in being accepted by a group of people who saw the world so differently from the way he did.

So why was he letting Shara's princess tone annoy him?

Royce wasn't sure. So he simply nodded and said, 'OK. I don't want you to answer the phone because if it *is* your ex then answering will give him what he wants. If you refuse to pick up you cut him off at the knees, so to speak.'

'Won't that make him mad?' she asked.

Royce smiled. 'More than likely. But who cares? It sounds to me like he's had his own way for too long. Now it's our turn. We're going to take control of the situation.'

He could tell from her expression that Shara was undecided about his approach, but by then it was too late. They both fell silent as the answering machine picked up the call.

There was nothing for one long minute, and then the phone was slammed down.

Shara winced.

Royce smiled.

The phone rang again almost instantly.

'Ignore it,' Royce said again.

This time Shara shook her head. 'I think I'd better answer it. It might not be him.'

'Then why didn't they leave a message?'

'I don't know. But there's one way to find out, and that's by answering the phone.'

'No. Not yet.'

'This is my home, not yours. I'll do what I like. You can't tell me what to do.'

Royce shook his head. 'This is your father's house, and he's put me in charge.'

Again it was too late for Shara to do anything. The answering machine picked up for a second time. The silence lasted for a couple of minutes this time, before the caller slammed the phone down again.

Royce watched Shara, who was studiously staring at her clenched hands.

Her hair really was magnificent. As dark as a raven's wing and as glossy as the finest satin. His fingers itched to touch it—so much so that he curled his fingers into his palms.

The curve of her cheek was exposed. The skin was milky-white, absolutely flawless and ridiculously vulnerable.

How a cheekbone could be vulnerable Royce wasn't exactly sure, but that was how it struck him.

The phone rang a third time.

Royce studied Shara carefully.

She was staring at the phone as if it was going to jump up and bite her.

Her body language was easy to read. It was painting a very different picture from what she'd told him that morning.

'You lied to me earlier,' he said, in a conversational tone that hid the anger tightening his gut.

He valued honesty above everything else. Not only did he see too much dishonesty in his line of work, but after what Fiona had done to him any form of deception was abhorrent to him.

Her head snapped around. 'I beg your pardon?'

Royce crossed one ankle over the other, rested his hands on his thighs. 'You said your father was over-reacting to the situation, but it's clear to me that you're terrified of your ex-husband.'

She looked startled, then wary. She issued a laugh that fell well short of being humorous, although he was pretty sure that was what she was trying to convey because she'd unclenched her fists and made a concerted effort to look relaxed.

'Nonsense,' she dismissed.

'It's too late to deny it. I believe what I see above what I'm told. My eyes don't lie, whereas people do. I saw your reaction just now.'

She tossed her head. 'What you saw is my frustration at being told not to answer the phone in my own home.'

Royce shook his head. 'Sorry, but I don't believe you.'

She looked about to say something, but at that moment the answering machine picked up.

Shara looked away from him, back to the phone.

Royce grew rigid in his chair as a male voice started speaking. Although *speaking* was a polite word for the filth that came spewing down the phone line.

Foul language and even fouler content.

About how he had no intention of letting Shara go. About the fact that he'd rather kill her first.

Royce tried to look past the surface stuff to the deeper meaning and intent beneath the words.

What he was listening to convinced him that Steve Brady was a sociopathic bully.

Bullying was all about power and control.

Bullies also typically targeted people who tended not to retaliate, who in fact responded in such a way as to feed their negative behaviour.

Which surprised him.

Shara was not that kind of person.

Their short acquaintance demonstrated that she gave as good as she got. He couldn't imagine her allowing herself to be bullied.

But then everything wasn't always as it seemed.

As he should know.

He'd fallen for a woman who'd pretended to be something she wasn't.

He knew first-hand that looks could be deceiving.

In Shara's case he'd seen her fear a moment ago.

It had been genuine. He would bet his career on it.

The question was: why was she pretending she wasn't?

There had to be a reason.

There was *always* a reason.

That was something he'd learned well before starting the Royce Agency. People always had a motive for doing something.

Royce rose to his feet.

Shara's head shot in his direction so fast he was surprised she didn't pull a muscle. 'What are you doing?'

'I'm going to talk to him.'

Her face showed alarm. 'Don't do that!'

Royce ignored her and picked up the phone. 'Brady...?'

The tirade was cut off mid-stream and replaced with screaming silence. Royce let the quietness drag on. He was used to situations like these, and immune to the resulting tension.

He doubted it was the same for Brady. No doubt the silence was playing havoc with the other man's nerves.

As he'd expected, Brady broke the silence first. 'Who is this?'

'My name is Royce. I'm a friend of Shara's.' He spoke calmly and confidently, although his voice hardened as he added, 'And I'm warning you to leave her alone or you won't like the consequences.'

His response was more silence. Uncertain silence. Obviously Brady was trying to come to grips with the sudden turnaround in events.

'My God! It didn't take the little slut long to move on, did it?' His voice was vicious. 'You're not the first, you know. Why don't you ask her just how many men she slept with while she was married to me?'

Royce frowned. If he ignored the content of Brady's words for a moment and concentrated on the way he spoke he would be able to learn a lot.

One, although his tone was vicious Brady had spoken more calmly than Royce would have given him credit for, given his previous tirade. And, two, Brady didn't wait for an answer but hung up the phone—softly.

Both of those things suggested he was very much in control.

Surely that hinted at the fact that Brady was telling the truth?

He'd seen enough musical beds in the homes of the rich and famous during his time running the Royce Agency to know that that kind of behaviour went on all the time.

It was an attitude that sickened him. Although he was no monk, and had had his share of women over the years—some might even say more than his fair share—Royce always remained faithful to the woman he was with.

For however long it lasted—which admittedly wasn't very long.

Why would he want to tie himself to one woman when there was a world of women out there to enjoy?

Back in his parents' day getting married and having children was the done thing. These days things were much more flexible. Some couples got married. Others chose to live together. And others remained single, either through choice or circumstance.

Royce planned on being one of the latter.

But while he *was* in a relationship he treated his woman with respect.

Royce glanced at Shara.

Beautiful, sexy Shara.

Maybe she *had* been sleeping around. Maybe that was why her marriage had turned sour.

It was possible.

But it didn't really matter.

He was a bodyguard, not the morality police.

Nothing excused Brady's behaviour. Abuse of any kind—whether it was verbal, emotional or physical—was inexcusable.

And what he'd just heard—both on the answering machine and during his conversation with Brady—convinced him that Shara had been abused in some way.

A wave of fury rode up his spine.

He was going to take a great deal of pleasure in bringing the other man to his knees.

'What the hell did you do that for?' Shara demanded as Royce dropped the phone back into its cradle.

Royce swung in her direction. 'I beg your pardon?'

Shara jumped to her feet and then wished she hadn't. She was so angry she was shaking, her heart beating nineteen to the dozen. 'You had no right to do that. No right at all.'

She began to pace, her sandals making a slap-slap sound on the tiles, then fading to nothing as she crossed the Aubusson rug.

Thoughts swirled through her head, one after the other, so fast they made her dizzy.

One thought stood out amongst all the others: all her hard work had just been undone in one fell swoop.

Anger ripped through her. Grinding to a halt in the middle of the Aubusson rug, she slammed her hands down on her hips and glared at Royce. 'Who gave you permission to butt your nose in like that? This is precisely the situation I wanted to avoid. You've ruined everything, damn it!'

Royce gave her a puzzled look. 'Perhaps you'd like to explain what it is you think I've ruined, exactly? Because I haven't got a clue what you're talking about.'

'Everything!' Shara raked a hand through her hair, unsurprised to find it was shaking. 'This is precisely the reason I didn't want a bodyguard in the first place. I don't need some stranger interfering in my business. This is *my* situation and I'll deal with it *my* way.'

Royce didn't look the least bit impressed by her outburst.

He was still standing by the phone. Still looking cool, calm and completely unruffled.

The fact that he was so in control while she was falling apart at the seams infuriated Shara no end.

'First, when he hired me to protect you, your father gave me permission to handle the situation *my* way. That's the only way I do business. He knows that. I have to have full control.' He folded his arms across his impressive chest. 'And, second, if what I've seen in the last twenty-four hours is any example of the way you've been dealing with the situation then it's entirely ineffective.'

Pressure built inside her head until Shara thought she was going to explode. She could hardly stand still, but at the same time found that her muscles were locked so rigidly tight she was incapable of moving.

Here we go again.

Another man telling her what to do.

Another man trying to smack her down.

Well, he could try. But he wouldn't succeed.

She glared across the distance separating them. 'How dare you? You conceited oaf! You've known me for all of two seconds and yet you're an expert on me and my way of dealing with situations? As far as I'm concerned your so-called expertise has just made the situation one hundred times worse. I don't care who you are. I don't care if you're one of my father's paid minions. From now on keep out of my way—or there will be hell to pay!'

Satisfied that she'd told him exactly what she thought of him, Shara spun on her heel and stormed out of the lounge room.

She stomped up the stairs to her bedroom and snatched up her handbag and car keys. She had no idea where she was going, but she had to get out of here.

How dare'd Royce put her down that way?

Frankly, she thought she'd done one hell of a job.

She was proud of the way she'd gathered enough courage to leave Steve. She was equally proud of the way she was ignoring his harassment.

It wasn't easy.

Turning the other cheek was damned difficult at times, but she was trying to let his behaviour bounce off her.

So Mr Just Plain Royce could put *that* in his pipe and smoke it!

Exiting the house via the back staircase, Shara breathed a sigh of relief when she reached the garage undetected. She slid the key in the car's ignition and was halfway down the driveway when she gave a victorious pump of her fist in the air.

She was no more than half a kilometre from the house when she stopped smiling. A glance in her rear vision mirror turned her smile into a frown.

There was a black sedan four or five cars back.

The same kind of black sedan that Steve drove.

Every time she made a turn the black sedan made a turn.

Every time she changed lanes so too did the other car.

Which, of course, could mean only one thing: Steve was following her.

Her teeth came together with an audible snap, and a shiver of fear snaked serpent-like down her spine.

'Oh, no,' she said.

Another quick glance in the mirror showed that the black sedan had closed the distance between them. It was now only three cars back, and getting closer all the time.

Her hands clenched on the steering wheel until her knuckles turned white.

'You stupid fool,' she muttered out loud.

When was she going to learn that making decisions in the heat of the moment always backfired on her? When was she going to learn that when she was emotionally upset she almost always made the wrong decision?

She'd accused Royce of making the situation worse not twenty minutes ago, and then what had she done?

Stayed in the house where she was safe?

Oh, no—not her.

She'd had to try and prove a point by sneaking out.

Had she thought of the possible consequences?

No.

Had she waited until she'd calmed down before deciding what her next step should be?

No again.

She hadn't just landed on the snake's head by accident this time; she'd jumped on it all by herself.

'Damn it. When will I ever learn?'

Royce peered through the front windscreen.

He'd been quite content to follow Shara at a distance. Close enough to intervene at the first sign of trouble, but far enough back to let Shara think she'd made a clean getaway.

It could prove interesting.

Where would she go? Who would she meet? What would she do?

The more he knew about her patterns of movement, her routine, the better prepared he'd be to deal with whatever the future held.

Information was power.

That wasn't supposition; it was fact.

But that attitude belonged to five minutes ago.

He'd abandoned the hang-back strategy thirty seconds ago.

For one simple reason.

Shara was being followed.

There was no doubt about it.

Every time Shara made a turn the black sedan several cars behind her also made a turn.

Every time she changed lanes the black sedan changed lanes.

Logic suggested this wasn't a random incident. Logic suggested that Brady had been watching the house and when Shara had left he'd followed her.

Cursing under his breath, Royce pressed the accelerator flat to the floor. The large 4WD leapt forward like a giant predator, gobbling up the grey ribbon of road beneath its tyres.

Thoughts whirred through his head at lightning speed.

Possibilities. Probabilities.

He assessed them all and came up with a strategy to counter each one.

Mixed in amongst all the analysing was a good dose of blinding fury. Not co-operating was one thing, but an outright attempt to evade him was quite another—and completely unacceptable.

The stunt Shara had just pulled reaffirmed his opinion of her.

Her actions were thoughtless and selfish, and he wouldn't put up with such spoilt, self-absorbed behaviour—a fact that he'd make quite clear when he caught up with her.

CHAPTER THREE

SHARA glanced in the rear vision mirror again. The black
sedan was right behind her. It was close enough that she
could see Steve's angry face framed by the front windscreen.

'What am I going to do?' she whispered.

Thoughts swirled through her head, but no obvious solution presented itself.

She glanced in the mirror again and did a double take.

Surely that was—?

But it couldn't be.

Could it…?

A big dark 4WD she hadn't noticed before was racing
down the road behind them.

She'd seen it before. Just last night.

Royce!

Royce was coming to rescue her.

Relief washed through her in waves.

She didn't care how he'd found her. All she cared about
was the fact that he had.

'Thank you, God!' she whispered. 'Thank you.'

What she needed now was a strategy. No more going off
half-cocked and landing in even deeper trouble. She needed
to think…and then she needed to act sensibly.

She could brake. That was one option. Royce would catch
up to her even faster. But what would Steve do?

At the moment he appeared content to sit on her tail rather than actually *do* anything. It was an intimidation tactic that was typical of Steve.

But if she slowed would he ram her with his car?

She doubted it.

This was a busy road. There was enough traffic to deter him from doing anything rash that could be witnessed and used against him. Unlike her, Steve thought before he acted.

Her other option was to pull over to the side of the road. That would force Steve either to stop or keep on going. If her car doors were locked and Royce was hot on their tail she couldn't get into too much trouble, surely?

Deciding the latter was the better option, Shara glanced in her side mirror and waited for a break in the traffic. Then, without indicating, she swung hard on the wheel and with a screech of tyres pulled over on the side of the road.

The blast of car horns that hit her eardrums suggested Steve had followed suit, but she waited until she'd brought her car to a halt before having a proper look.

Steve was right behind her.

He was getting out of his car.

Shara started to shake. Her hands grew sweaty. Her heart thumped.

The sight of her ex-husband was enough to make her feel sick and anxious. It was a feeling she remembered all too well. It dominated her consciousness, blotting everything else out.

With a squeal of tyres another vehicle screeched to a halt beside her. A quick glance showed her it was the big 4WD.

Royce.

He ignored the fact that he was blocking one lane of traffic and jumped from his vehicle.

Her relief was so strong that Shara fumbled for the door latch and did the same.

Royce looked so big and solid. So reassuringly safe.

Without thinking, she flung herself at him. 'Boy, am I glad to see you!'

Strong arms closed around her.

Shara was aware of heat and the smell of warm male skin. She was also aware of the strength and power barely contained in the muscled lines of his body.

Cocooned against Royce's chest, Shara felt safe and secure.

She also felt something else.

A ripple of desire.

It was the first time she'd admitted, even to herself, that that was what the curling sensation in her belly she experienced every time she looked at him was all about.

Now she had no choice but to acknowledge it.

It packed quite a punch.

Enough to make her push away from him.

She was just over-reacting to their close proximity and to the adrenalin pumping through her system.

That was all.

It was nothing personal.

If she told herself that often enough she might even believe it.

Royce clasped her wrists and pulled her hands down from around his neck before she could completely disengage herself.

'Stay there,' he said, dragging her behind him so that he stood between her and Steve.

Nothing more was said.

Not a single word.

The air was filled with menace. Filled so completely that it raised the hairs on her arms and the back of her neck.

She could feel Royce's body braced for action, but it wasn't needed. She heard the scuffle of footsteps, the slamming of a car door, and then the screech of tyres as the black sedan raced off, leaving behind a trail of exhaust smoke and the smell of burning rubber.

As soon as Steve had disappeared Royce turned, a heavy frown on his face. Gripping the tops of her arms, he gave her a brief hard shake before putting his face next to hers. 'You little fool. Sneaking off like that was stupid and reckless. What on earth were you thinking?'

Shara blinked, her heart leaping into the back of her throat.

Royce was angry.

Very angry.

Steve had looked at her the same way many times.

Now, as then, she shrank in on herself—both physically and mentally. Her shoulders hunched, her muscles contracted, her breath shortened.

The grey, smoke-filled fog of fear closed around her like a shroud. Suffocating. Deadening. Numbing.

'I…I'm s…sorry,' she stammered. Inside she cringed at how apologetic she sounded. She hadn't heard that particular tone of voice come out of her mouth since she'd been with Steve. 'I wasn't thinking.'

Shame washed through her.

She didn't want to revert to the woman she'd been when she'd been with Steve.

The reasons for staying in an abusive relationship were many and varied, and had nothing to do with the victim's character or strength of will.

It had taken Shara a long time to come to terms with why *she'd* stayed with Steve.

One reason was that she hadn't wanted to admit that marrying Steve had been a mistake. Her father had been against the marriage. He'd told her she was rushing into things. She hadn't wanted to admit that he'd been right.

But the driving force—the thing that had compelled her to stay—was fear.

Crippling, disabling fear.

Steve's threats had quite literally paralysed her into inaction for a long time.

She'd been terrified he'd become more violent if she tried to leave.

Terrified that he'd come after her.

And those fears had proved to be justified, because that was exactly what he'd done.

She dragged in a breath, and then another. Slowly her heartbeat began to return to normal. Her fear began to recede. The smoky fog was washed away.

And her power of thought began to return.

She didn't want to be that frightened woman any more.

She *wouldn't* be that woman any more.

She'd come a long way since then. The last thing she wanted to do was backtrack.

OK, so her marriage to Steve had conditioned her to respond negatively to certain things.

But she could rise above it.

She could *un*-learn it.

Somehow.

Starting now.

Royce stared at Shara. Saw the fear in her eyes and realised *he* was responsible. Heard the stammer in her voice and knew that he was answerable for that too.

Immediately his heart stilled.

He was a fool.

A stupid, thoughtless fool.

He'd scared the poor girl half out of her wits. As if she hadn't already been scared enough.

Taking a deep breath, he relaxed his hold on the tops of her arms and adopted a calm expression. His hands soothed gently up and down. 'It's OK, Shara. I'm sorry I yelled at you.'

She didn't look at him. She was staring downwards.

'I wasn't thinking,' Royce continued. 'I didn't mean to frighten you.'

She was shaking, her breathing coming in short gasps.

'That's it.' Royce deliberately kept his voice low and even. 'Take some deep breaths. In and out.'

Gradually she stopped shaking.

'That's it. You're almost there,' Royce encouraged.

Finally, Shara lifted her head. 'Let me go!'

Royce immediately did as she asked. In fact he went one better. He took a couple of paces backwards. His behaviour had obviously made her feel threatened. Giving her some space would help put her at her ease.

It was important Shara felt safe with him—not just because it would be easier for him to do his job, but because he was not a man who got his kicks out of frightening women. He'd leave that kind of behaviour to the likes of Brady.

'That's it,' he said, relieved to see that her breathing was becoming calmer and deeper. 'You're going to be all right.'

Shara dragged in another calming breath and glared at him. 'All right? I doubt very much if I'm going to be *all right* if you're going to go on creating situations like this one.'

He pointed a finger at his chest. 'You think *I* created this situation?' he asked incredulously.

'I certainly do.'

'And just how do you figure this is my fault?'

She tossed her hair over her shoulder. 'You deliberately provoked Steve on the phone earlier.'

'And how did I do that?'

'You told him you were a friend of mine, and—'

Royce nodded. 'I did. What's wrong with that?'

'Apart from the fact that it's a complete and utter lie, you mean?'

He nodded. 'Apart from that.'

'What you don't know is that Steve is insanely jealous—to

the point of being completely paranoid.' His paranoia had become so bad that she'd had to walk on eggshells all the time. 'All I had to do was talk to a man and Steve thought we were having an affair. And if a guy so much as looked at me Steve was ready to beat him to a pulp.'

'And how am I supposed to know that when you refused point-blank to discuss it with me?' he flung at her, but without his earlier aggression.

Shara tossed her head. 'I didn't want to discuss it any more than I wanted you interfering. But it's too late for that. You've already stuck your oar in and muddied the water.' She dragged in a breath. 'Telling him that we're friends has probably given him completely the wrong idea.'

Again, Royce nodded. 'If it's any consolation, you're right. He accused us of sleeping together.'

Shara gasped, lifting her hands to her cheeks. 'Oh, no! That's terrible. Just terrible.'

'Why is it terrible?'

'Are you mad?' she gasped. 'Haven't you listened to a word I've said?'

He shook his head. 'No, I'm not mad. I'm perfectly sane. And, yes, I've listened to everything you've told me.'

'Then surely it's obvious why I'm so upset?' Her mouth twisted. 'Steve won't like the idea of me being with someone else, that's why! Even if it isn't true.'

Royce had an odd look on his face. 'OK. Let's leave that for a moment. You were about to add something else a minute ago when I interrupted you. What was it?'

Shara frowned. 'You threatened him. How on earth do you think *that* will help the situation?'

'If he has any sense he'll listen to my advice and forget about you, and the situation will be over.'

She barked out a harsh laugh. 'And if he doesn't—and I'm betting he won't—you'll have just made him angry.'

'So?'

So.

One word. Two letters. Simple.

Only it wasn't simple.

Royce had used the word in the context of *So what?* a term normally given in answer to an unimportant or irrelevant statement, indicating indifference on the part of the speaker.

Well, that was all well and good for Royce.

But he hadn't lived in her world.

If he had he'd know that there was nothing indifferent about making Steve angry. If anything, the exact opposite was true—which was precisely why she was so concerned.

Shara wrapped her arms around herself, chilled to the bone.

'It doesn't pay to make him angry,' she whispered.

His expression shifted. It was a subtle thing. It was as if all the muscles in his face had hardened. 'What happens when you make him angry?'

Shara shook her head, tremors making their way up and down her spine. 'He retaliates.'

'He hit you?'

Shara hugged herself even more tightly. 'Once.' She paused for a heartbeat. 'But there are other ways of making someone suffer.'

Although she didn't think it was possible, his face hardened even more.

'I know there are,' he said grimly. 'I'm sorry you had to go through that.'

Shara wasn't sure whether it was the unexpected sympathy or the memories that got to her, but suddenly tears were stinging the backs of her eyes and clogging her throat.

Royce muttered a curse under his breath, pulled her against his chest and wrapped his arms around her.

And suddenly a few tears became a flood.

A flood she couldn't seem to stop.

Her arms slid around his waist as she buried her nose against his chest and cried for all she was worth.

Royce spoke softly to her. She didn't hear a single word. Not one. But the sound of his voice and the rumble in his chest when he spoke was soothing.

Finally she pulled back with a loud sniff. She stared at his shirt and the large patch of damp fabric in the middle. 'Sorry about that. I've made your shirt all wet.'

'Don't worry about it. It will dry.' He looked around. Cars were whizzing by them. 'Let's get out of here.'

She nodded.

But neither of them moved.

They stood staring at each other.

The atmosphere changed. Deepened.

His head began to descend towards hers. Of its own volition her mouth lifted.

And then, suddenly, they were more than a foot apart.

Shara wasn't sure who moved first. Royce or her. Either way, it didn't matter.

Didn't matter because what had almost happened shouldn't have happened.

Royce cleared his throat. 'We need to talk—but not on the side of a road.'

She sniffed again. 'There's nothing to talk about.'

Not about the near-miss kiss. Not about her crying jag. Or anything else for that matter. Her position hadn't changed. Just because Royce had rescued her from a potentially sticky situation it didn't mean she'd changed her mind. She still didn't want him interfering.

Royce frowned. 'Yes, there is. We need to talk about our strategy for handling your case going forward.'

Your case.

Those two words were a harsh reminder that his concern wasn't personal. He was just doing his job.

She knew that.

Of course she did.

So why was there a distinct pang in the centre of her chest?

Shara moved away from the heat and the smell of him. She wiped a hand across her eyes, removing the last traces of tears. 'I repeat: there's nothing to talk about. You're just making the situation worse. Don't you understand that?'

'That's why you didn't want a bodyguard?'

She nodded. 'I want you to butt out. I can't make it any clearer than that.'

Royce folded his arms across his chest and stared her directly in the eye. 'Oh, you're being crystal-clear. Have no doubt about that. But that is precisely the reason we need to talk.'

Shara frowned. 'I don't understand.'

Royce sighed and reached out, fleetingly touched her cheek with his fingertips. It was the lightest of touches, and lasted for barely a second, and yet it had a rippling effect right through her system.

'I know you don't.' His tone was odd. 'And therein lies the problem.'

'Stop talking in riddles,' she ordered.

'OK. You don't like my approach to handling your ex?'

Shara shook her head. 'No, I don't. It's too confrontational. You're just going to escalate the situation. And I won't have that. I *won't.*'

'You may just have to, because—'

Shara stamped her foot. 'Because nothing. I don't care whether my father hired you. I don't care what his instructions are. This is *my* life, and I'm done with everyone interfering.'

Royce stared at her long and hard. His chocolate-brown eyes were veiled but at the same time penetrating. Finally he said quietly, 'No, you'd rather continue to play the victim.'

He might as well have hit her. Her head went back. Her heart leapt into the back of her throat. A shudder so deep and penetrating that it rocked the lining of her soul ripped through her.

She staggered back from him. 'You take that back. You take that back right this minute,' she gasped, barely able to get the words out through numb lips. 'I'm not playing at anything. I *am* the victim.'

Royce inclined his head. 'You *were* a victim. It's your choice whether you continue to be one or not.'

Her hands clenched and unclenched. 'If I were a man I'd hit you into the middle of next week for saying that. I made a choice not to be a victim the day I left Steve.'

'Then why aren't you fighting back?'

He asked the question softly. Somehow that had far more impact than if he'd shouted.

'I *am* fighting back,' she said, but her voice was little more than a whisper.

His eyes didn't waver from hers. 'How? Tell me that.'

The words were blunt and to the point. They attacked without mercy.

Shara blinked, an unsettled feeling attacked the base of her spine. 'I left him.'

Royce waved a dismissive hand. 'I'm not denying that, but what have you done since then?'

'I—' She snapped her mouth closed. 'Well, I—'

What *had* she done?

Her mind sifted through the catalogue of her actions since Steve's harassment had begun and she didn't like what she was seeing. Ignoring his behaviour, turning the other cheek, avoiding going anywhere she was likely to run into him. Not exactly fighting actions, were they?

'Everything you say and everything you do regarding your ex-husband is submissive. It's as if you've chosen a course of passive resistance where he's concerned.' His eyes bored into hers, serious and determined. 'You don't want to be confrontational because it will make him angry and if you make him angry, then he'll retaliate. You're feeding his power over you. Can't you see that? You're letting him keep control. If you don't break that pattern of behaviour nothing will ever change. He'll always have a hold over you.'

Shara stared at him and kept on staring.

The breath was locked in her lungs so tightly they felt as if they were going to burst. Her heart was beating so fast and so hard she was sure her ribs would crack at any moment.

He was right.

She didn't want to admit it, but he was.

It was as if Royce had stripped away an invisible veil that had prevented her from seeing her own actions clearly.

'God, I'm such a fool,' she said, burying her face in her hands.

Royce grasped her wrists and pulled her hands away from her face. 'No, you're scared. I understand that. Fear does strange things to people. No doubt you've become conditioned to react the way you have.'

She released a bitter laugh. 'You're right. I thought I was being tough and strong by ignoring Steve's harassment. But I can see now that all I've been doing is what I learned to do during my marriage.'

'Which is?'

'Keep the peace. Don't provoke. Play it safe. The only difference between now and then is that I've been doing it long-distance.'

'Don't beat yourself up over it. It's perfectly understandable.'

She snorted. 'You think?'

He nodded. 'I *know*.'

'I think you're being overly generous, but thank you for saying it.'

'Don't thank me. I never say anything I don't mean. What you need to do now is focus on the future.'

Shara hadn't allowed herself to think too much about the future because Steve's harassment had chained her to the past. Now, for the first time, she had a glimpse of a future in which she was free and in control of her own life.

As if reading her mind, Royce said, 'Keep in mind that the dynamic has changed. *I'm* involved now. That adds an entirely new dimension to the situation. The bottom line is that you don't have to be scared any more. I won't let anything happen to you. I'll keep you safe.'

Shara stared up at him, an emotion she couldn't quite define sweeping through her. 'I want to believe you. I really do. But you don't know what he's like.'

Royce shrugged. 'I don't need to. I've dealt with some pretty tough characters in my life.'

'Still—'

'Still nothing. I'm an expert. Brady isn't. He doesn't stand a chance against me. I *will* protect you. That's a promise.'

Shara wanted to believe him. Wanted to believe him so badly that she could taste it.

But that meant placing her trust in a complete stranger.

Her trust *and* her safety.

But what choice did she have?

'Trust me,' Royce urged, as if he sensed all the doubts swirling around in her head.

She nodded her head jerkily.

'Truce?' Royce asked, holding out his hand.

'Truce,' Shara said, taking his hand.

A tingle of something that felt very much like electricity shot up her arm. As it did so a disturbing thought jumped to the forefront of her brain.

Royce might protect her from Steve, but who was going to protect her from Royce and the magnetism that had burst to life between them?

Royce wanted Shara to return to the house with him, but she refused.

'If you're worried about your car, don't be,' he said. 'I can have someone come and pick it up.'

Shara shook her head. 'Why put someone else to the trouble when I'm already here?'

Why indeed?

Royce had to admit that her attitude grated on him—but for all the right reasons.

Fiona had had little or no respect for her father's household staff. She'd dropped clothes willy-nilly on the floor and had left towels in the bathroom in much the same way.

The fact that Shara hadn't jumped at his suggestion hinted that she was different.

It was only a little thing, admittedly, but Royce had learned that a person's values were reflected in *everything* they did—both the big and the small.

Shara's response just didn't gel with his initial impression of her.

But then his impression of her was changing all the time, wasn't it?

When the household security system—a system *he* had personally installed—had alerted him to the fact that Shara was sneaking out of the house, he'd been furious.

Stupid and *thoughtless* were two of the more polite words that had sprung into his mind. So too were *irresponsible* and *reckless*.

The stunt she'd pulled had reinforced his opinion that she was spoilt and self-absorbed, but their conversation just now forced him to acknowledge that that wasn't entirely true.

Shara had refused a bodyguard out of a misdirected sense of self-preservation. Scraping back the surface had revealed a woman who was strong and courageous.

Because it took courage to admit when you were wrong.

And it took courage *and* strength to face your fears.

And that was exactly what Shara was doing.

She might have gone about it the wrong way, but she *was* trying.

He couldn't help but admire her for that.

'Coffee, I think,' Royce said when they entered the house. 'Unless you'd prefer something stronger?'

Shara shook her head, sending her hair swirling around her shoulders. 'I don't need anything stronger. I'm not going to fall apart on you again.' She smiled a twisted kind of smile. 'One meltdown a day is my limit.'

He laughed, pleased that she wasn't taking herself too seriously. 'You didn't have a meltdown. You just—'

'Had a meltdown,' she said dryly.

Whatever it was she'd had, she'd regrouped marvellously. He shrugged. 'Everyone has a release valve that goes off occasionally. That's what keeps us sane.'

'I can't see *you* bawling your eyes out.'

Royce grimaced. 'I must admit I prefer hitting the gym.'

'Maybe I'll think about doing the same thing next time.' She picked up the kettle. 'How do you take your coffee?'

Royce told her, and watched as she bustled around the kitchen.

She moved with an easy grace that obviously came naturally. It was a pleasure watching her move about.

'So, if you don't hit the gym, what do you do to relax when the pressure is on?' he asked.

'Listen to music,' she replied promptly.

'What kind?'

She shrugged. 'Nothing too heavy. I like pop and light classical music. If I close my eyes I can lose myself in a song. It's a great way to escape—if only for a little while.'

Royce remembered the way Shara had been swaying and twirling to the music the previous evening. He cocked an eyebrow. 'Is that what you were doing in the club last night? Trying to escape?'

She grimaced. '*Trying* being the operative word. Except I kept getting interrupted. First by Tony and then by you.'

'Tony is the guy you gave short shrift to?'

She plonked a mug down in front of him with more force

than necessary. The coffee rolled around the edge of the cup but somehow managed not to spill.

'That's a rather cutting remark,' she said, taking a seat opposite him.

'I'm just calling it as I saw it,' he returned unapologetically.

He'd been on the receiving end of that kind of dismissal once before and he knew how it felt. Fiona had laughed in his face for thinking she'd ever been serious about him. That laugh had cut him to the quick.

'Well, for your information, Tony has been making a nuisance of himself. He won't take no for an answer. Last night I had to tell him straight to leave me alone.'

'I see,' he said, digesting this new piece of information and realising that it put a different slant on the scene he'd witnessed.

'Or are you one of those guys who thinks that no means yes?' Shara asked, breaking in on his thoughts. 'Because if you are then we're not going to get on at all.'

Royce held up his hands. 'Not me. No means no in any language. I have a strong sense of right and wrong. It's one of the things that led me to starting my business.'

'Good.' She tapped her fingertips on the tabletop. 'If Tony had two brain cells to rub together he would have backed off earlier. The ink is barely dry on my divorce papers. My ex is still harassing me. The last thing I want is to get involved with someone else. Is that so hard to understand?'

Royce shook his head. 'Not at all. In fact it's perfectly understandable.'

Royce remembered how he'd felt when he'd discovered Fiona had betrayed him. He'd been sure he'd never get involved with a woman again.

He had, of course.

Sex was a powerful motivator. He had no intention of living the rest of his life like a monk.

There was, however, one major difference.

Since Fiona he had always maintained a cool distance emotionally in all of his relationships.

If he'd been using his head back then he would have known that something wasn't quite right about their relationship. In fact, he'd have known there was something downright fishy about the whole situation.

If he'd had his wits about him he'd have seen through the web of lies and deceit and seen Fiona for exactly what she was—someone who was using him for her own ends.

At the time he'd thought her interest in him—and the case—was sweet. Instead all she'd been doing was pumping him for information—both literally and figuratively.

'You say that as if you're speaking from personal experience,' Shara commented, breaking in on his thoughts.

'I am. I doubt that any man—or woman, for that matter—reaches the grand old age of thirty-four without having been burned once or twice.'

She raised one neatly plucked eyebrow. 'Once or twice?'

Royce stared back. 'Once. I always learn from my mistakes.'

CHAPTER FOUR

SHARA was staring at him, a mixture of sympathy and sadness in her eyes.

Royce ignored the former, but the latter made his heart constrict.

Such a young and beautiful woman shouldn't have so much sadness in her eyes.

Royce wanted to take her hand in his and say something—anything—to banish that unhappy look.

To make her smile.

Or laugh.

It wasn't an appropriate reaction—just as almost kissing her by the side of the road earlier hadn't been appropriate.

He stared deeper into her eyes and saw a question burning there. It was clear she wanted to ask him more about what had happened, but he had no intention of trading war stories.

He hadn't even told Travis and Jackson, his two closest friends, what had happened with Fiona. The last thing he wanted was anyone feeling sorry for him. The important thing was that even though he'd been hurt at the time the experience had provided an invaluable life lesson.

Getting involved warped your viewpoint.

Emotions fuzzed your objectivity and made you vulnerable.

He'd acted like a stupid fool with Fiona, but—as he'd just

told Shara—he'd learnt his lesson and had no intention of re-peating the same mistake twice.

Something in his expression must have warned Shara not to pursue the subject, because after taking a sip of her herbal tea she said, 'You mentioned that having a strong sense of right and wrong led you into starting your business?'

Royce grasped the change of subject with both hands. 'Kind of. To be honest, I had a whole other career mapped out. I was going to be the world's next Bill Gates. The secu-rity business picked me rather than the other way around.'

She raised an eyebrow. 'And how did it manage to do that?'

Royce rubbed the side of his jaw with his fingers. 'I've always had a thing about supporting the underdog. I guess it came from being bullied as a child.'

'*You* were bullied? I find that hard to believe,' she said, making no attempt to hide her incredulity.

'Why?'

Shara blinked, then waved a hand towards him. 'You just don't look the type.'

'Because I'm big?'

She nodded.

'Big doesn't necessarily mean aggressive, you know.'

'I suppose not.'

'Strange as it may seem, my size was one of the reasons I was picked on in the first place. I was taller than everyone in my class. A couple of the other kids assumed that because I was big I was also tough. They decided to see just how tough I was.'

'You mean…?'

He nodded. 'They decided to fight me whether I wanted to fight or not. I hated it.'

'I can imagine,' she said.

'After I'd been beaten up a few times my dad decided we'd better do something about it.' His smile was rueful. 'He en-rolled me in a local karate class. I never looked back.'

'So instead of getting beat up you did the beating instead? Why do men always have to be so macho? Surely there was a better way of dealing with the bullies than meeting violence with violence?'

Royce shook his head. 'You have it wrong. Martial arts training gave me confidence. I wasn't scared any more. And because I knew what I was doing I could dissuade most of the bullies without hurting them. Strange as it may seem to you, I actually abhor violence.'

'You sure picked a strange profession, then.'

He grinned. 'Not really. My business is mostly about prevention. I can't stop other people from behaving aggressively, but I can protect others from being hurt. Which is exactly what happened at school.'

Shara frowned. 'I'm not following you.'

Royce picked up his cup to prevent himself from reaching across and smoothing the small furrows on her brow with his fingertips. 'If I saw another kid being picked on I stepped in before the situation went too far. I made it clear to the bullies that they'd have to deal with me if they did anything.'

'And did they heed the warning?'

'Some did. Some didn't,' Royce replied, taking a sip of coffee.

Shara raised an eyebrow. 'And the ones who didn't?'

'Let's just say that they didn't need a third warning,' he said simply, his gaze steady on hers.

Shara drew away from him, looking horrified. 'What did you do to them?'

He frowned at her reaction and leaned across the table. 'I think you've got the wrong end of the stick. If you're imagining bloody noses and broken bones then you couldn't be more wrong. I don't operate that way. The only thing that got injured was their pride.'

'I see.'

'I hope you do. Because the last thing I want is for you to think that I'm some kind of thug.'

Not only was his professional reputation important to him, so was his personal one. A man should protect his character as solidly as he protected himself.

Shara shook her head, sending her hair swirling around her shoulders. 'How could I think that after what you did this morning?'

Royce frowned. 'You've lost me. What did I do this morning?'

'When you got angry you reminded me so much of Steve that you frightened me. As soon as you realised what was happening you immediately backed down.'

Royce still didn't get the point. 'I did. So?'

She smiled an odd kind of smile. 'Steve would never have done that. He seemed to enjoy scaring me.'

The admission made him grit his teeth as a wave of fury rode up his spine. It nauseated him to think about what Shara had had to endure.

Royce took a deep breath, surprised by the depth and intensity of his reaction. He'd dealt with numerous sleaze-buckets over the years—had witnessed more sordid and downright awful situations than he cared to think about. But he accepted them as part of the job.

It was a fact of life that those things existed.

There was no point getting emotional about it. Doing so was just a waste of time and energy and achieved nothing.

Instead, he dealt with ugly situations the same way he dealt with everything.

With discipline and self control. And with calm, cool logic.

So why the hell was he sitting here wanting to smash something at the thought of what Shara had had to endure?

Royce wasn't sure, but his reaction set alarm bells ringing.

'Unfortunately I'm not surprised. These guys get their rocks off pushing other people around.' He curled his lip. 'But you don't have to worry about that. Be assured that Brady won't touch you while I'm around.'

Shara stared at him with big wide eyes, 'I think I'm beginning to believe you.'

Shara could hardly believe those words had come out of her mouth, but they had.

Royce's confidence was reassuring. So too was the strong sense of justice he'd just been talking about.

But talk was cheap. Actions always spoke louder than words—and the way Royce had come to her rescue this morning, paired with the way he'd backed down when he realised he was frightening her, were ample evidence that he meant what he said.

She could, she was beginning to realise, trust Royce—at least to some extent.

She pushed her empty mug away. 'It's still a big leap from dealing with a couple of schoolyard bullies to operating your own business.'

He flashed her another of those bone-melting smiles that made her heart turn over. 'I know. In fact it's a bigger leap than you can even imagine.'

'Go on.'

'My career transformation started when I was hauled up to the headmaster's office one day and accused of hacking into the computer network to change the grades of some of the students.'

'But you didn't,' she said without hesitation.

Royce raised an eyebrow in her direction. 'You sound very sure.'

'A man with a strong sense of justice wouldn't cheat like that.'

'Well, your instincts are right. I had nothing to do with it.'

'So what made them accuse you?' Shara asked, resting her chin on her cupped hands.

It was only human nature to be curious about someone you were going to be sharing a house with for the foreseeable future, Shara assured herself. It wasn't as if she was interested in him or anything like that.

'They had no proof, if that's what you're asking. Their excuse was flimsy, to say the least.' She gave him an enquiring look. 'They thought I was the only student capable of hacking into the system.'

'Obviously you weren't, since it was someone else.'

He nodded. 'Exactly. I can understand why they thought it was me, though. I have a knack for computing. Since it was one of my subjects they knew that. Still, I was furious at being unjustly accused with so little evidence.'

'I can imagine.'

It was the kind of injustice that Shara could understand. When Steve had first turned on her shortly after their wedding she'd been bewildered. But quickly on the heels of her confusion had come the question: What have I done to deserve this?

'So guess what I did?' Royce asked.

The question dragged Shara back to the present. 'I wouldn't have a clue.'

'I offered to find out who the hacker was,' he said, with the same panache as someone pulling a rabbit out of a hat.

Shara sat back in her chair. It was an idea that hadn't even occurred to her. 'That's a unique solution—but how on earth could you do that?'

'Actually, it was quite easy. The hacker was an amateur compared to me, so tracing him wasn't difficult.' Royce pushed his chair back from the table and crossed an ankle over a knee. 'But it gave me the idea that maybe it would be challenging, not to mention more interesting, doing that kind of thing for a living instead of straight computer work. So I decided to find out. I approached a well-known security company to see if they'd give me a part-time job.'

It was a logical step, although Shara very much doubted it would have occurred to *her*. 'And did they?'

'No, they laughed in my face. They thought it was hysterical that a schoolkid thought he had something to offer them. But that was a mistake.' Another of those heart-melting smiles flashed across his face. 'What they didn't realise was that, one, I don't like being laughed at, and, two, defeat is not a word in my vocabulary.'

Shara was beginning to realise that—which meant that he was a good man to have on her side. 'So what did you do?'

He leaned conspiratorially closer and beckoned her to do the same with a crooked finger. He waited until she'd pushed her cup aside and leant across the table before saying softly, 'I hacked into their computer system.'

Shara almost choked on her own tongue. 'You didn't!'

Royce nodded. 'I most certainly did. I left a message in the inbox of every employee of the company telling them that if they didn't hire me they'd regret it.'

Shara stared at Royce open-mouthed, then threw her head back and laughed. Not a delicate little giggle but a full-on belly laugh. She couldn't remember the last time she'd laughed like that.

Finally she sobered. 'I shouldn't be laughing. That really was very naughty of you.'

'I know. But do you blame me?'

Shara thought about that. 'I suppose not. Although with your sense of right and wrong I'm surprised you didn't think you were crossing the line.'

'Considering there was no malicious intent involved and that I signed my name to the e-mail, I figured I wasn't doing any harm other than proving that I was determined.'

'Oh, I think you managed to prove that,' she said dryly.

'The company obviously thought so too.'

Shara frowned. 'Don't tell me they threatened you with the police?'

Royce shook his head. 'No. In fact just the opposite. They were on the phone the next day with all kinds of offers.'

Again it was an answer she hadn't been expecting. 'Are you sure you're not making this up?'

'Scouts' honour,' Royce said, giving her the three-fingered salute that usually accompanied the saying. 'It takes quite some skill to bypass the security of a security company, you know.'

'I hadn't thought of it that way, but I suppose it does.' Not only was he determined, he was clever right along with it. 'Did you accept?'

'Of course. I worked with them through the rest of high school, learning the ropes and the various aspects of the business. Then, while I was at university, I started my own business.'

'And now you're the largest and most well-known security firm on the globe?'

'The biggest and the best,' Royce said proudly.

Shara frowned. 'I was less than gracious the last time we discussed this. I apologise. Obviously your success is well deserved.'

'Thanks, but your apology isn't necessary.' He pushed his mug away. 'Now, enough about me. Let's discuss our strategy moving forward.'

'Do we have to?' Shara demanded. 'I'm sick to the back teeth of talking about Steve. I don't even want to *think* about him.'

'I'm sure you don't. But we need to go over a couple of things. After that we won't mention Brady again unless we absolutely have to. Deal?'

'All right,' she agreed reluctantly.

Royce stared at her for a long moment. There was something about the lack of expression on his face that made the hairs on the back of her neck stand on end.

'I want you to take out an Apprehended Violence Order against Brady,' he said quietly.

Shara frowned. 'I've heard of them, but I'm not sure how they work.'

'An AVO is used to protect a person against both acts of violence and the threat of violence. It covers everything from physical assault to non-physical abuse, such as harassment or intimidation. The order itself doesn't give a person a criminal record, but the clincher for us is that a breach of the order *is* a criminal offence.' He leaned forward. 'If Brady crosses the line once the AVO is in place we can have him arrested.'

Shara shook her head even before he'd finished speaking, her hands clenched tightly together in her lap. 'I don't think that's a good idea.'

Royce frowned. 'Why?'

'Because it's too confrontational, that's why.'

Royce stared at her—hard. 'I thought we'd already had this conversation. Don't tell me you're back-pedalling already?'

Shara bit down on her lower lip. 'I'm not back pedalling. I'm just…'

He raised a brow. 'Just what?'

'Exercising caution.'

Royce sighed and leaned across the table. 'Well, I hate to tell you this, Shara, but caution just isn't going to cut it.'

She read the determination written on his face. It was unsettling. 'You're serious about this?'

He nodded. 'I am. Very serious.'

Shara gripped the edge of the table. 'What you're suggesting is suicide.'

'No, it's not. Brady can't touch you without going through me first.'

Shara eyed the rock hard muscles of his shoulders and arms.

Of all of the things Royce had said to her—the promises and assurances—what he'd just said was the most reassuring. If Steve came up against Royce it would be like pitting a domestic cat against a lion or a tiger.

Royce was a professional.

He'd proved that more than once.

Maybe it was time she started listening to his advice.

She nodded before her courage deserted her. 'OK. I'll do it.'

'Good. I'll get Jackson on to it right away.'

'Jackson?'

'Jackson Black. He's a friend of mine and a very good lawyer,' Royce explained. He paused for a moment, then asked, 'Can I take it that you'll co-operate from now on? There'll be no more incidents like the one this morning?'

Shara nodded.

'Good. We have a much better chance of success with us both working together.'

Shara grimaced, not so sure she wanted to work together with Royce.

After that near-miss kiss earlier, working together could prove altogether too dangerous.

'What is it?' Royce demanded when he saw her grimace.

'Nothing. I'm just being stupid.'

'I'll be the judge of that.'

She shrugged. 'When I left Steve I promised myself that I'd stand on my own two feet.'

'You are.'

She shrugged again, drawing his attention to her breasts. 'It doesn't feel like it. Not when I'm relying on you to protect me.'

'Give yourself a break, Shara,' Royce said, speaking in no uncertain terms. 'No one is completely self-sufficient. If you have a leak you call a plumber. If you have car trouble you take it to a garage. If you're sick you go to a doctor. There's nothing different about this situation. You're being threatened and I'm an expert at protection. End of story.'

'I suppose so.' She paused. Looked away then back again. 'How long do you think this is going to take, anyway?'

She rested her elbows on the edge of the table. The action squeezed her breasts together, deepening her cleavage in the low neckline of the white T-shirt she was wearing. Royce found it difficult not to stare. In fact he found it impossible not to.

She had a fantasy-filled bra. He was a man who liked curvy women. Maybe it was because he was such a big man himself. Skinny women did nothing for him. Somehow he knew Shara's breasts would fill his hands perfectly, and his fingers itched to pull off her T-shirt and bra and discover the truth for themselves.

As he watched her nipples tightened to beads under the thin fabric. She'd noticed him staring and her body was reacting.

Suddenly the air around them was filled with electric tension.

His eyes shot to her face. She was staring at him, twin stripes of colour flagging her cheeks.

The realisation that she was being turned on by his look sent a surge of hormones racing through his body. His erection was hard and fierce and instantaneous beneath the zippered seam of his trousers.

Shifting on his seat, he willed his body under control.

He didn't want to be attracted to Shara. Not only was she the principal, but she was cut from the same mould as Fiona.

Both came from rich families and both had been raised by doting fathers who had spoiled them rotten at every turn. The result, of course, was that they were selfish and self-centred. They took more than they gave.

Royce preferred women who'd forged their own path in life the same way he had. They could be models or lawyers.

It didn't matter. All that mattered was that they appreciated what they had because they'd earned it, and that they respected others because that was how it was meant to be.

'This?' he asked, focussing his attention on the conversation at hand.

'Yes, *this*.' She waved a hand through the air. 'You being here? Getting Steve off my back?'

'That depends.'

'On what?'

With a shrug of his massive shoulders, Royce drew his long legs out from under the table and lifted one leg to cross an ankle over a knee. 'On lots of things. Each case is different, I'm afraid. I can't tell you when it's going to end.'

'Surely you must have some idea?' she asked, sounding desperate.

'I'm afraid not. But we're about to change the rules. That might be enough to make Brady back off.' He stared at her, a cold feeling invading his insides at what he was about to say. 'Or it might not. It might make the situation worse—just as you feared.'

She paled.

Royce didn't want to frighten her. She'd already been frightened enough. But he had to lay his cards on the table. It was only fair that she knew what to expect.

'I hope not,' she gasped.

'I hope not too. But being forewarned is being forearmed. If he does anything once we've taken an AVO out against him then we'll have him,' Royce said with satisfaction.

He'd love nothing better than to see the other man in jail.

There was nothing new about that. He believed in justice. He liked to see the bad guys get their comeuppance. It was one of the reasons he'd started the Royce Agency in the first place.

So his reaction was perfectly normal.

Except it wasn't.

There was something different about this situation.

Something different about his reaction.

It was subtle, but it was there.

And, whatever it was, he had the terrible feeling that it had something to do with the woman sitting in front of him.

'How I wish I had your confidence,' Shara said with a sigh, her fingertips making circular patterns on the top of the table. 'I'm tired of being scared.'

'Well, if you feel that way maybe you should do something about it,' Royce suggested.

'Like what?' she asked, curious in spite of herself.

She would do anything not to be scared any more.

To feel safe.

Free.

'Why don't I give you some karate lessons?'

It was the last thing she'd expected him to say. She barked out a laugh and waved a dismissive hand through the air. 'I don't think so.'

'Why not?'

She stopped laughing. 'You're serious?'

He nodded. 'Of course I am. I happen to believe everyone—particularly women—should know the basics of self-defence. The world isn't a safe place. Things happen. People end up in the wrong place at the wrong time. They should know how to protect themselves. Knowing you possess those skills will give you confidence. There have even been studies showing that by projecting that confidence you're less likely to be attacked in the first place.'

Shara stared at him doubtfully. 'I'm not very athletic.'

'You don't have to be. I'm not talking about turning you into a black belt who can take on ten men at one time.'

'I should hope not,' she said, with another laugh.

At the same time a quiver of sensation swept through her. It was all too easy to imagine Royce taking on ten men—

and winning. She could imagine his muscles rippling as he moved. Could imagine the gleam of danger darkening his chocolate-brown eyes to black.

'All I'm talking about is teaching you a couple of moves that will get you out of trouble. You'd be surprised how effective a few simple blocks and punches can be.'

Blocks and punches?

He had to be out of his tree.

Shara shook her head. 'Thank you for the offer, but I don't think I'd be any good at it.'

He stared at her for such a long time that Shara began to feel uncomfortable. 'What?' she demanded.

'Attitude is nine-tenths of battle. If you want confidence then you need to start acting confidently. Don't admit defeat before you've even given it a try.'

Shara stared at him. 'What is it about you? Are you a bodyguard or a psychologist?'

He shrugged. 'I little bit of both, I suppose. An amazing amount of what I do involves getting inside other people's heads. I guess some of it rubs off.'

She cocked her head to one side. 'I also have the sneaking suspicion that you don't believe in wrapping things up in cotton wool.'

Royce shook his head. 'No, I don't. I don't see any point in beating around the bush. I call it as I see it. So, how about it? Are you up for the challenge?'

Shara shrugged. 'I can't very well say no now, can I?'

His eyes gleamed. 'You could, but you wouldn't be talking the talk or walking the walk.'

'I know. I know. If I want confidence then the first thing I have to do is act confident.' She thumped her hands palms down on the table. 'OK. I'll give this karate gig a try. What do I have to do?'

His eyes skimmed over her. 'The first thing you have to

do is change. Put on something that's loose-fitting and comfortable. And lose the sandals.'

Shara shrugged. He was the expert. He obviously knew what he was talking about.

She climbed the stairs to her room and did as he suggested, finding a pair of loose-fitting white trousers she usually wore over her swimsuit to the beach. She left her white T-shirt on. It was stretchy and comfortable so it should fit the bill.

They reconvened in the lounge room.

As she entered Shara's mouth ran dry.

Royce had also changed. He was wearing a pair of black loose-fitting cotton pants and a singlet that bared the steely strength of his broad, bronzed shoulders to her hungry gaze.

She came to a skidding halt just inside the doorway, her heart beating like a runaway train and her mouth so dry she had to lick her lips to moisten them.

If she'd had reservations about this karate lesson before, one look at Royce quadrupled them.

She hadn't given the physical aspect of Royce's suggestion any thought.

Now she did.

She was going to have to touch him.

He was going to have to touch her.

Already she was more aware of him than she wanted to be.

To use one of his own phrases, karate now sounded much too 'up close and personal' for her liking.

Royce saw her at that moment. His eyes ran over her, a gleam in their depths suggesting he approved of what he was seeing.

'Good, you're here,' he said, waving her further into the room.

Shara smoothed her moist palms down over her curvy hips. 'I'm really not sure about this.'

He raised one thick, dark eyebrow. 'You're not chickening out on me, are you?'

It was a challenge and they both knew it.

Courage.

That was what she needed.

And loads of it.

What had he said before she'd agreed to this insane suggestion?

Yes—that was it.

Talk the talk and walk the walk.

So that was what she did.

She dragged in a breath, walked into the room, and said, 'No, I'm not chickening out.'

Royce studied Shara as she walked into the room. She'd followed his instructions and changed into a pair of white loose-fitting pants which were partially see-through.

Not completely—just enough to make the outline of her shape visible.

And what a shape it was.

Lush. Curvy. *Womanly*.

Hormones raced crazily through his system, hardening muscles and other parts of his anatomy.

Suddenly he regretted offering to give Shara karate lessons.

He'd trained many people over the years—women included. He'd also had numerous sparring partners. He knew what was involved.

Being close.

Touching.

Normally those things didn't bother him.

Today they did.

Which was ridiculous.

He was a professional, not an amateur.

He knew the importance of separating his personal feelings from the job at hand.

There was no doubt in his mind that he could get through this session with the same cool aplomb he would have if he was teaching a man.

He'd pushed some of the furniture back and put the coffee table in a corner of the room, leaving the entire Aubusson rug free for them to work on.

Before he could change his mind Royce went and planted his feet in the middle of the rug, right in front of Shara.

'OK, let's start with some simple blocking techniques.'

Shara was so close he could smell the scent of her fragrance. She'd pulled her hair back into a high ponytail on the back of her head. Although he preferred her with her hair down, the ponytail highlighted her spectacular bone structure and made her eyes appear bluer than blue.

'The first block I'm going to show you is a lower block. It's used for blocking both strikes and kicks.'

Shara nodded. 'OK. Where do we start?'

'Watch me. I'll show you how it's done first.' He braced his feet shoulder-width apart, then put his right arm by his side and tucked his left arm up under his shoulder. 'This is the starting position. Then, leading with your elbow and forearm, move the left arm across your chest, blocking your middle area. At the same time swing the right arm in a circular motion, protecting the lower area.'

Royce demonstrated the movement several times.

Shara stared at him with studied concentration, eyes slightly narrowed, a furrow forming between her brows.

'Now you try,' Royce suggested.

Shuffling her feet into position, Shara moved her arms into the starting position. 'Is this right?'

'Yes—now have a go at the block.'

Shara tried, but her arms tangled. 'I'm sorry. I did it wrong.'

She sounded almost anxious. 'Don't worry about it. Hardly anybody gets it right the first time. Here, let me help you,' Royce said, moving even closer.

Then he did what he'd been dreading and anticipating all at the same time.

He touched her.

CHAPTER FIVE

SHARA dragged in a breath. When she'd mucked up the move she'd tensed, half expecting Royce to yell at her.

Only he hadn't.

Instead he'd dismissed her error with barely the blink of an eye.

Which wasn't what she was used to.

Steve had shouted at her all the time.

If the spaghetti sauce she'd made wasn't thick enough he'd bellowed at her as if it was the end of the world. If it was too thick he'd bawled her out just as loudly. If the bed wasn't made tightly enough to make a coin bounce he'd criticised her, and if his shirts weren't ironed to absolute perfection there had been hell to pay.

The constant stream of abuse and the barrage of insults had resulted in her living in an almost constant state of anxiety.

It would take some time getting used to this new state of affairs—but she was looking forward to it.

Royce stepped towards her. He was so close she could feel the heat radiating off his body and smell the scent of his soap or deodorant.

Her nerve-endings twitched as if they'd just been plugged into an electrical socket. Her skin was taut and tight, as if it were being stretched over her bones.

And then he touched her.

Shara tried not to jump. She really did. But she wasn't sure she was entirely successful because Royce gave her a sharp glance.

'Get into the starting position again,' he instructed.

Was his voice deeper than it had been a minute ago? Huskier?

Shara snuck a peek at him through the shield of her lashes. He was staring at her cleavage in a way that instantly made her nipples tighten.

Starting position?

The only positions that sprang into her head had nothing to do with karate but came straight from the pages of the *Kama Sutra*!

Forcing her attention back to the task at hand, Shara adopted the starting position.

Royce placed one hand on her left upper arm and the other on her left wrist. 'OK, relax.'

Relax?

Who was he kidding?

She had as much chance of releasing her tensed muscles while he was touching her as she did of flying to the moon.

'Let me guide you through the movement.'

His hands moved on her arms, leading her step by step.

He would be a good lover, Shara decided, trying to ignore the touch of his hands on her skin. He would lead her to a mind-bending climax with the panache and precision of a conductor conducting an orchestra.

Theoretically speaking, of course.

Because she wasn't the least bit interested on a personal level.

Definitely not.

Although it *did* make her wonder about the woman Royce had been in love with. The one who had hurt him.

What had *she* been like?

And what had gone wrong between them?

'OK. Repeat the movement with that arm only.'

Shara blinked. She felt like an idiot. She'd been too busy imagining what kind of lover Royce would be and hadn't concentrated on what he'd shown her.

Shara tried the movement again—and got it wrong.

'I'm sorry,' she said.

'Stop apologising. It isn't necessary,' Royce said.

He sounded totally normal. That deepening of his voice had either been her imagination or just a momentary something-or-other.

He was fine now.

All business.

She might as well be a department store dummy for all the effect she had on him.

Whereas *her* system felt as if it was going to go into complete meltdown.

'Lead with your elbow across your body,' Royce instructed.

Shara tried again—and got it wrong. The words *I'm sorry* were sitting on the tip of her tongue, but she swallowed them back.

'Again,' Royce instructed.

She did it again.

'Better.' He paused for a beat. 'Again.'

She repeated the move half a dozen times until Royce was satisfied.

'Good.' He nodded his approval. 'Now let's do the right arm.'

His hands were on her again. Confident and sure. By the time she'd mastered the right arm movement to Royce's satisfaction she was hot and more than a little bothered—and it had nothing to do with the lesson and everything to do with Royce.

'Now let's put it together.'

They worked for an hour on two closed-fisted blocks, the jab and the elbow strike.

By the time they finished Shara was exhausted—and strangely satisfied.

How could a few simple moves make her feel strong and powerful?

Shara wasn't sure. Maybe it was the endorphins that had been released into her bloodstream as a result of exercising, or maybe it was simply a psychological reaction to doing something positive and proactive in case she needed to defend herself.

Either way, that was exactly what had happened.

'So, what did you think of your first lesson?' Royce asked.

Although she'd enjoyed it immensely, Shara was reluctant to say so.

Because the truth was that it wasn't just the karate she'd enjoyed but the touching too.

And therein lay the problem.

She was playing with fire.

And fire tended to burn.

She'd been burnt before…and she didn't want to be burnt again.

Shara was taking such a long time answering that Royce tensed—although why that should be the case he had no idea.

Her answer shouldn't matter to him one way or another.

Although that wasn't quite true.

If anything, he should be hoping that she'd hated their session and had no desire to repeat it.

That would be the safe outcome.

Safe…?

Oh, yes.

Definitely safe.

Because the opposite was…

Well, it was fraught with danger.

Shara was the principal. He was the bodyguard. He should maintain a professional distance.

But, despite what common sense demanded and professional etiquette dictated, Royce still hoped that Shara would say, *Yes, I liked it and I want to do it again.*

Because *he* wanted to do it again.

Not just the karate, but the touching too.

Which was just not on.

He knew better than to get involved with a client—particularly a rich woman like Shara. They always had their own agenda, and what they wanted was usually at the centre of it.

All he had to do was think about how Fiona had seduced him to suit her own ends to know that.

Although comparing Shara to Fiona wasn't entirely fair, Royce admitted reluctantly.

Shara's situation was pretty straightforward and her agenda was clear: make her ex stop stalking her.

Shara was also quite a different kettle of fish from Fiona—as he was beginning to discover.

Today had been pretty intense. He'd put Shara on the spot more than once. In every instance not only had her reaction been genuine but she'd risen to the occasion beautifully.

Still, alarm bells were ringing, and if there was one thing he'd learned it was to listen to his instincts.

He opened his mouth to retract his offer to give her more lessons, but before he could get a single word out Shara spoke.

'It was great.' She sounded strangely breathless, and there was a look in her eyes that made his hormones go ballistic. 'Maybe we can do it again some time?' she suggested casually.

Royce couldn't explain what happened when he heard her answer. He should have been disappointed. Should have said he'd changed his mind.

But he did neither of those things.

He really did believe that it was important for Shara to learn self-defence.

It was a legitimate reason for continuing with the lessons. He wasn't justifying it.

And it certainly had nothing to do with Shara personally.

He raised an eyebrow and said, equally casually, 'How about tomorrow?'

The next day was Sunday. As well as practising what he'd taught her the day before, they worked on two more blocks, and a punch as well as a kick.

They were almost at the end of the lesson when Shara folded her arms and shook her head. 'I can't do that. I might hurt you.'

Royce laughed.

She loved it when he laughed. It was a deep, rumbling sound that created an answering vibration deep inside her.

'You won't hurt me,' he denied. 'I'm bigger and stronger than you are.'

Oh, yes, he was bigger and stronger—and absolutely gorgeous with it. A fact that had been in her face throughout this session. There was something incredibly sexy about the hard contours of his body that made her not only want to look, but to touch too.

'That may be so, but I'd still prefer to keep practising that kick in the air,' she said.

Royce let the cushion he was holding drop to his side. 'Kicking in the air is OK to get an idea of the movement, but it's impossible to develop a powerful or useful kick that way. You can only learn how to generate power and speed by kicking something solid.'

Still she hesitated.

'Come on, Shara. It's important. Women have stronger legs than arms. I want you to know how to kick properly.'

She sighed. 'You're going to make me do this, aren't you?'

He nodded. 'Yes, I'm going to make you do this. And there's not a snowball's chance in hell that you're going to hurt me, so forget about it.'

Shara stared into his face. Concern and stubbornness were a potent mixture, she decided.

For the first time she registered just how much Royce was going out of his way to give her these lessons.

Her hands dropped to her sides. 'Do you know I haven't thanked you for doing this?'

'You don't have to thank me.'

'Yes, I do. You're investing time and effort helping me when you could be doing other things.' She paused for a heartbeat, emotion clogging the back of her throat. 'It's a long time since anyone has done that for me.'

Royce frowned. 'I find that very hard to believe.'

'I don't know why you should. Dad is a workaholic who can barely give me the time of day. Steve is a taker not a giver. The only thing he's ever given me is grief, and I hardly think that counts.'

Royce's frown had deepened. 'I'm sure you have friends that—'

Shara waved a hand. 'Steve made it very difficult for me to make new friends, and my old crowd—the ones that I was at the club with the other night… Well, let's just say I've outgrown them. Anyway, I just want you to know that I appreciate what you're doing for me.'

Royce stared at her long and hard. 'You're welcome. You can show your gratitude by kicking me.'

Shara laughed. 'That's sneaky.'

'I know. That's something you should remember about me. I'll use any tactic to get my own way. So—into position.'

Shara waited until Royce was holding the cushion braced in front of him and then she kicked.

Royce lowered the cushion. 'What a wussy kick! Surely you can do better than that?'

Shara stared at him, noting the teasing glimmer in his eyes and the half-smile tilting his lips.

She leaned her weight on her back foot and then flashed him a smile. 'You want harder? I'll give you harder.'

Pushing off her back foot, she snapped her leg forward and kicked the cushion as hard as she could.

Royce absorbed the impact, his muscles bunching as he braced his body. 'That was excellent! Whoops!' he said as she stumbled against him.

She'd kicked so hard the momentum had carried her forward—straight into Royce.

She landed against his chest.

His arms closed around her.

She looked up.

Their eyes met.

Romance novels were full of what they called 'moments frozen in time'.

Shara had never quite understood what they meant.

Now she did.

The world faded. Shrank until nothing existed but the two of them.

There was no past.

There was no future.

There was just this one moment in time.

And then it was gone.

Just like that.

As if the present had been snuffed out and the world had restarted with them standing several feet apart.

This time there was no question about who had moved first.

Royce had.

He'd turned away, breaking eye contact and shattering the spell that had bound them together for that brief instant.

What Shara found so disconcerting was the fact that she *hadn't* moved.

She'd just stood there.

Waiting to be kissed.

Because certainly that was what had been about to happen.

Why had she just stood there, waiting for him to kiss her as if that was what she wanted?

Because it wasn't.

Was it…?

Her breath hitched and her heart thumped when she realised that she wasn't quite so sure of her answer to that question as she should be.

By mutual consent their karate sessions and the break they shared together afterwards became a daily event.

Shara looked forward to it almost as much as she dreaded it.

'I'm enjoying the karate more than I ever imagined I would,' Shara told Royce several days later. 'I didn't think I would, you know.'

'Why not?'

Shara shrugged. 'I guess because I've never exercised much. But I like the way it makes me feel.'

The karate workouts had given her a new-found appreciation for working her body. Everything from the feel of her muscles expanding and contracting to the sense of co-ordination she felt as the different parts of her body moved in sync.

There was also a sense of achievement associated with mastering a new movement or refining her technique. It was a feeling she hadn't felt since high school, when she'd done well at exams.

'I know what you mean. After a session I always feel more—well, *balanced* for want of a better word.'

Shara nodded her agreement. 'And you were right. I *do* feel more confident. Not quite ready to take on ten men at one time, but I think I could get out of trouble should the need arise. Given what I went through with Steve, that's a pretty big deal.'

'I'm sure it is. You should be really proud of the progress you've made,' Royce said, flopping down on the sofa. 'You're doing amazingly well for a beginner.'

'Thanks. You've made it easy. You're a good teacher.'

And he was.

He was patient and supportive. When she was struggling to master a new move he worked with her, using encouragement and praise instead of criticism and disapproval to achieve the desired results.

'I try.'

That was something else she'd noted about Royce. He was modest. Although he was successful, and had the kind of ultra-confidence that oozed out of every pore, he didn't have a big head.

'You do more than try. You succeed.' Shara hesitated a moment, and then said, 'I wanted to be a teacher, you know.'

'No, I didn't know. What stopped you?'

'My father. He thought it was a waste of time.'

Royce was clearly surprised. 'Why? I would have thought he'd be pleased you'd chosen such a worthwhile career.'

She laughed, but there was no humour in it. 'The only career a woman should have, according to my father, is to be a wife and mother.'

Royce was so clearly gobsmacked that it took him several minutes to answer. 'You have to be kidding. That is…'

'What? Archaic? Primitive? Antiquated? All of the above?'

'Definitely all of the above.' He shook his head. 'I don't know what to say.'

'I know the feeling. That's exactly how I felt when my father started talking about it. He explained how important it was for me to make the right choice. He wanted me to marry someone from a wealthy and reputable family. Someone who would help him expand his business empire. In other words he wanted to marry me off as some kind of a business trans-action. He even had a list of potential candidates. He didn't care what I wanted. As far as he was concerned he knew best. He *always* thought he knew what was best for me.'

'So that's why you married Brady,' Royce said thought-fully, phrasing the remark as a comment rather than a question.

Shara barked out a laugh. 'I'm afraid not. Steve doesn't come from a wealthy or well-known family.'

'So he was an act of rebellion?' Royce asked.

She shook her head. 'Nothing so dramatic, I'm afraid. If I'd wanted to rebel I'd have gone to university like I wanted to. My mother left me a trust fund. I'm sure the trustees would have released the funds for an education, even if it was against my father's wishes.'

'So you married for love instead of duty?'

Shara frowned as she thought about that. 'If you'd asked me that at the time I'd have said yes, but now I'm not so sure. If you want to know the truth I don't think I ever loved Steve.' She was saddened by the admission. It was another of the many mistakes she'd made. 'I think I latched on to him because I was desperately looking for a way to escape my father. What I didn't realise was that I was jumping straight from the frying pan into the fire.'

'I can't argue with that. Brady is obviously some piece of work.'

Shara scratched the side of her head. 'Do you know I never realised how similar Dad and Steve are until just now? Obviously Steve is a far more extreme case than my father, but they both like using threats to get their own way. Do you remember that first night, when you brought me home from the club? You said that my father had asked you to tell me that while I'm living under his roof I'm to follow his rules. He said that so often when I was growing up that I got sick of hearing it.'

'I'm sure he meant well,' Royce said tactfully.

Shara shrugged. 'Maybe he did. I'm not sure. All I know is that he made me miserable in the process.'

Shara stared at Royce. He was so different from the other men in her life.

He wasn't a bully. He didn't browbeat her to get his own way. Nor did he take pleasure in putting her down.

But, much as she liked and respected him for those and other qualities he possessed, there was still one thing she couldn't get past.

He liked things done *his* way.

Royce had told her so himself—more than once.

On the night he'd brought her home from the club he'd told her that he had to have full control, and during one of their karate lessons he'd admitted that he'd use any tactic to get his own way.

Well, she'd had enough control to last her a lifetime. She wanted the freedom to make her own decisions.

Which was precisely why she had to ignore her attraction to Royce.

There was only one role she wanted him to play in her life—and that was her bodyguard.

On Friday they were so absorbed in their lesson—and in each other, although Royce didn't want to think about that—that they worked for almost two hours.

'OK. I think that's enough for the day,' Royce said, finally calling a halt. 'You've done well.'

Her arms dropped to her sides. 'I could do with a glass of water. Do you want one?'

Royce nodded and followed her to the kitchen. As usual, he enjoyed watching her move about.

The phone rang. Royce reached out a hand and picked up the receiver. 'Hello.'

When there was no response he said hello again. His answer was silence.

Out of the corner of his eye he could see Shara watching him.

These phone calls happened every one or two days. If he answered there was always silence. But there was no mistaking the waves of animosity coming down the line.

If Shara answered the response was mixed. Sometimes there was silence. Sometimes there was the traditional, if uncreative, heavy breathing. At other times she was hit by a barrage of abuse that made her slam the phone down.

Royce had discreetly had the phone records checked. All the phone calls came from payphones. Shara didn't recognise the voice, but the tinny sound suggested whoever was calling was using a voice-changer.

'If that's you, Brady, then listen up. Shara doesn't want to see you. She doesn't even want to talk to you. So leave her alone.'

This time he didn't wait for a response. He slammed the phone down with the secret hope that it would give the other man a headache.

'He's never going to give up,' Shara said, plonking a glass of water down in front of him.

Every time one of these calls arrived the shadows reappeared in her eyes—something that made Royce more and more angry.

Royce grasped her hand. 'Of course he is. Don't let these calls get you down. That's exactly what Brady wants. Don't give him the satisfaction.'

She squared her shoulders. 'You're right. I'm done with letting him have power over me.'

Royce grinned. 'That's my girl.'

Shara nodded and took a sip of her drink. Royce watched her lips close around the glass. Watched her head tilt back. Watched the movement of her throat as she swallowed.

Dragging his eyes away, Royce took a long slug of water.

'I have a question for you,' Shara said.

'Shoot.'

'How do my appointments fit into your super-duper protect Shara strategy?'

Royce put his glass of water down. 'What sort of appointments are we talking about?'

'I do charity work.'

She might as well have said that she did magic tricks. Or rode to the moon on a bicycle.

Neither was more astonishing than what she'd actually said.

Although why he should be so surprised he wasn't sure. Plenty of women did charity work. He just hadn't figured Shara would be one of them.

It was dawning on him—slowly—that the image of her he had fixed in his head was wrong. Cracks the size of elephants were appearing in his mental vision.

Why he hadn't seen it sooner Royce had no idea. The truth had been staring at him almost from the beginning.

The courage Shara had demonstrated in leaving Brady and trying to deal with his harassment on her own touched him deeply. It wasn't often that you met someone—man or woman—who had to face the kind of things that Shara had had to face.

He'd also thought she was spoilt.

Huh!

What a laugh that was.

Perhaps financially she'd been spoilt, but she'd been starved of her father's attention which was far worse. And in a clear demonstration of her inner strength neither of those things had had a detrimental effect on her character.

Royce realised he was guilty of pigeonholing Shara without any evidence to back up his opinion. He'd made a superficial, not to mention sweeping comparison of Fiona and

Shara's backgrounds and immediately shoved them into the same category.

But he'd been wrong—on all fronts.

To date Shara had proved herself to be stubborn and determined, honest and open.

Royce stared at her and realised Shara was still talking. He tuned back in to the conversation just in time to hear her say, 'On Monday I have a meeting with some people regarding the planning for a charity ball which is their main fundraising event of the year. It's not the kind of thing I'd like to cancel.' She paused for a heartbeat. 'This particular cause is close to my heart.'

Royce gave her an enquiring look.

'My mother died of ovarian cancer,' she said huskily.

'I'm sorry. How old were you?'

'Twelve.'

His heart contracted. 'There's never a good time to have a parent die, but I imagine twelve is one of the more difficult ages.'

Shara nodded. 'Especially for a girl. Mum and I were close. Her death left a huge gap in my life. My father didn't know what to do with me.'

Given what he knew of Gerard Atwood, Royce could imagine that a grieving near-teenager would have been a challenge for him.

'Well, there's no need to cancel. I'll simply come with you.'

Shara was frowning.

'What is it?' Royce asked.

She shrugged. 'How will I explain you being with me?'

'You can explain it however you like. Although I suspect telling the truth will only make you—and them—uncomfortable. Why don't you just say I'm a friend who's going to lend a hand?' He paused for a moment. 'It's not too far from the truth, you know. I do a bit of volunteering myself.'

'You do?'

He nodded. 'The Royce Agency runs a free anti-bullying programme for schools called Kid Power.'

'Because you were bullied as a kid?'

He nodded. 'It's a cause close to my heart—just as the ovarian cancer charity is close to yours.'

'Well, in that case I'd love to have you come along.'

'Are you sure you wouldn't rather wait outside?' Shara asked on Monday, stopping on the pavement outside the building that was their intended destination.

'I can't do that,' Royce said. 'Up close and personal, remember?'

After their recent karate lessons Shara was beginning to think they were already *too* up close and way, *way* too personal.

'Royce, it's an office building. I'll be surrounded by people. What could happen to me here?'

'Plenty.' Royce folded his arms. 'Brady could have followed us here.'

'But he didn't, did he? I noticed the way you kept on checking the rearview mirror on the way here.'

The fact that he was so vigilant was reassuring. He really was a consummate professional. But above and beyond that she also knew he was a caring person who would do whatever he had to do to protect her.

'I don't think he did,' Royce said. 'But protecting someone is about not taking chances. And don't forget I thought I saw him watching the house a couple of days ago.'

Shara hadn't forgotten. Even though Royce wasn't one hundred percent sure it had been Steve—the guy had been wearing a baseball cap, sunglasses and an oversized jersey—it had still been depressing news.

Royce waved to the building behind them. 'There are multiple entrances and exits in this place. I can't cover all of them.

Brady could simply walk in and confront you. I'm not taking that chance.'

He was right. It was better to be safe than sorry. 'OK. Let's go.'

They rode up in the lift in silence. Shara announced their arrival at Reception, and they were shown into a meeting room where the other attendees had already gathered.

Noreen, the committee chairperson, came up to them. Before Shara had the chance to make introductions Noreen jerked her head towards Royce and asked, 'Who is the mountain?'

Straightening her spine, Shara raised herself to her full height. Once she might have let a comment like that go. Now she wouldn't.

Steve had loved putting her down. He'd seemed to get some kind of perverted pleasure out of doing it.

Back then she'd been too frightened to defend herself. Now she wasn't. At least not with someone like Noreen.

'Don't be rude, Noreen,' she said.

'No offence intended,' Noreen said, glancing at Royce.

'None taken,' Royce said.

The fact that he sounded amused rather than annoyed didn't alter the fact that Shara was pleased she'd said something.

It made her realise how far she'd come.

The Shara she was today wouldn't put up with half the abuse Steve had given her.

If a man didn't like the spaghetti sauce she'd made she'd tell him to like it or lump it.

If the bed wasn't made tightly enough to bounce a coin she'd tell a man to make it himself.

The realisation was...

Well, it was liberating.

It was as if a physical weight had been lifted off her.

She actually felt lighter—as if she were floating several feet above the floor.

She introduced Royce to the other attendees before taking a seat.

Royce sat down beside her.

Their thighs brushed under the table. Shara jerked her leg away. 'OK. Let's get started, shall we?'

Noreen opened the meeting with a progress report on what had been achieved since the last time they'd got together. Shara tried to concentrate, but found Royce's presence a distraction.

'OK. Let's move on,' Noreen said. 'I'd like to focus now on the prizes for the auction. Do we have any volunteers who are willing to contact the people who donated prizes last year and see if we can persuade them to provide something again this year?'

'I'm happy to do that,' Shara said.

'Excellent.' Noreen pushed a sheaf of papers across the table. 'Here are the names and phone numbers, plus a list of what they donated. Given the state of the economy, I suspect we're not going to get them all back on board—which means we need to spread our net wider. Any suggestions?'

'I'm happy to donate a free security assessment of someone's home and make recommendations on what they need to do to resolve any deficiencies,' Royce said. 'I'm also happy to contact a few of my business associates to see if they'll donate something.'

'Excellent, excellent,' Noreen said. 'Anyone else?'

'You didn't have to do that,' Shara whispered to Royce as several other people pitched in with suggestions.

He shrugged. 'I'm happy to do it. As I said yesterday, I'm more than willing to support a good cause.'

'Still, it was nice of you to do it.'

And she didn't want him to be nice, because that just made him even more attractive.

CHAPTER SIX

ROYCE leaned back in his chair and watched as Shara addressed the meeting.

She was formally dressed, in a classic white suit and a black silk blouse, with subtly applied make-up, a French braid, and simple gold jewellery.

She looked elegant and businesslike—and so beautiful that she took his breath away.

Still, he much preferred her the way she was just after one of their karate lessons. A little dishevelled, with strands of hair escaping her ponytail, her eyes sparkling like a gazillion sapphires.

With difficulty he forced his attention back to what she was saying. She was currently outlining the programme for the actual event itself.

She was talking about serving times and collection times and break times. When the music would start and when it would finish. At what time the auction would begin and what time it would end.

It was clear she'd put a lot of time and effort into the event. It was also clear she'd done this before. She knew exactly what she was doing—expertly fielding questions as they arose, clarifying the finer details when required.

Royce found himself as captivated by this side of Shara as he was by the woman he'd already come to know.

* * *

When the meeting had been concluded they made their way to the lift.

'I hope you didn't mind me getting involved in the meeting?' Royce asked, pressing the 'down' button.

'Why would I mind?'

He shrugged. 'A bodyguard should be seen and not heard. Even then he should only be seen when he needs to be. It's my job to blend into the background.'

Shara laughed out loud. She couldn't help herself. 'I don't think it's possible for *you* to blend into the background.'

'Too much of a mountain?'

Too much of everything!

Good-looks. Sex appeal. Charisma.

For a second Shara was afraid she'd made the comment out loud. The answer had flashed into her head so quickly her brain hadn't had the chance to edit it.

But Royce was looking at her so normally she couldn't have.

'I'm sorry about the comment Noreen made,' Shara offered, the incident still rankling.

Royce shrugged. 'It's water off a duck's back. I've been called worse things in my time, and no doubt I'll be called a good many more.'

'Still, she shouldn't have said it.'

'Forget it. I have.'

'OK.'

At that moment the lift arrived with a soft *ping*. The doors slid open. Royce held an arm across the opening to prevent the doors from closing and then waved her inside.

Shara walked past him.

Her arm brushed against his.

A shot of electricity flashed up her arm.

Her eyes flew to his.

What she saw in his eyes made her heart stop.

* * *

Royce followed Shara into the lift.

The air was locked tight in his lungs. His heart was doing the exact opposite, loosening up the floodgates and sending his blood rushing from one end of his body to the other with supersonic speed.

Instinct had always served him well. Several times it had even saved his life.

This time it abandoned him. Dumped him smack-bang in the middle of a place he shouldn't be.

Because, without thinking, Royce bent his head and claimed her mouth with his. He kissed her as if he'd been waiting years to kiss her instead of days.

As his mouth plundered hers Royce admitted what he hadn't wanted to admit until now: he'd wanted her from the first moment he'd seen her, swaying so sensually on the dance floor.

And the crazy thing was that Shara was kissing him back the same way. With not a second's hesitation and enough hunger to set his pulse flying.

Royce fed a hand into her hair. He held her head steady as his mouth continued to move over hers.

Her hands clutched at his chest, grabbing a fistful of his shirt.

Even that small amount of contact was enough to make his senses go haywire. Desire was zinging off the inside of his skin and sending a shudder through his tall frame.

It was an amazing feeling.

The rush grabbed him.

Held on.

Wouldn't let him go.

Wherever the rush was going, he was on board for the ride.

Shara went up in flames the minute Royce's mouth claimed hers.

There was no other way to describe it.

She could feel the heat.

Feel it scorching through her, stripping her of everything but the truth.

She wanted Royce.

There. She'd admitted it.

The stomach-curling sensation and the electrical charge that literally zapped through her body every time they touched was good old-fashioned sexual desire.

Lust.

It pounded through her.

Minced her resistance into a pile of mush.

Flattened her common senses into non-existence.

Thought vanished.

All that was left was sensation.

A wild uproar of sensation that lifted her to her toes and made her cling to him as if she never wanted to let him go.

It didn't matter that what they were doing was wrong.

The part of her consciousness that recognised that fact had gone into hiding.

The *ping* of the lift sounded again. Awareness of where she was, who she was with and what she was doing came flooding back.

She sprang backwards, almost falling over her own feet in the process.

The world rushed back at her so fast that she felt dizzy. For those few extraordinary moments it was as if all of her focus had converged on Royce.

His mouth.

His arms.

The feel of his body against her.

Now she slowly turned her head.

Two men were standing in the opening of the lift, grinning at them.

Mortified, she dropped her chin towards her chest.

She was aware of Royce turning, and then he said with a hint of humour, 'What floor?'

Shara cringed inside.

What was wrong with her? Wasn't her life complicated enough without getting involved with someone else?

Royce glanced at Shara as the doors slid shut behind the two guys, who had got off on the fourth floor.

She was standing as still as a statue, her body visibly tense. Her hands were clenched at her sides so hard that the knuckles had turned white.

So far she hadn't said a single word to him.

Royce wasn't even sure that she'd looked at him.

As if she sensed his eyes on her, she turned on him, her eyes spitting blue chips of ice. 'What on earth did you do that for?'

It was a good question.

A *very* good question.

Because the honest-to-God truth was that he *hadn't* been thinking.

When her arm had brushed against his all rational thought had flown straight out of the window. Instinct had made him reach for her.

Instinct...and desire.

Oh, yes. He couldn't forget that.

The desire had risen up inside him, grabbed him in its tenacious grip and simply refused to let him go.

'Well? Answer me!' Shara ordered, reverting to the imperious, hoity-toity tone of voice she hadn't used for some time. 'Do you always try to kiss your clients?'

She had a knack for going straight for the jugular.

'No, I don't,' Royce replied calmly, watching her with dark narrowed eyes. 'In fact, I make it a rule not to mix business with pleasure.'

'Really?' She tossed her head and flung her hand in the air. 'Then what was that…that *fiasco* all about?'

She'd done it again.

Put him right on the spot with another pointed question.

A question that he had no answer to.

His gut shrank to the size of a pea.

A *fiasco*…?

She thought their kiss was a *fiasco*?

Hardly.

He could think of any number of descriptions to describe the conflagration that had taken hold of them, but a fiasco would not be one of them.

'You enjoyed it as much as I did,' he accused.

Royce wasn't sure exactly where those words had come from. He certainly hadn't intended saying them.

What he *should* be saying was that their kiss had been a mistake and one that wouldn't be repeated.

But Royce always told it the way it was. Even if the truth was unpalatable, it still needed to be said.

Shara blinked her big blue eyes at him, her expression suddenly guarded. 'No, I didn't.'

'Yes, you did.'

She blinked again. Her mouth trembled. 'You're imagining things.'

Royce shook his head.

This was the first time he could remember Shara trying to dissemble—and she wasn't doing a very good job of it.

Desire was surging up inside him again. The rush of it made his head spin.

Instinct took over a second time.

He did two things simultaneously.

He took a step towards her and he slapped a hand against the emergency stop button.

The lift came to a jerking, juddering halt.

Shara took a stumbling step backwards. 'What…what do you think you're doing?'

Those blunt questions just kept right on coming—as if they were bullets fired from a gun.

What *was* he doing?

Royce wasn't sure, but he knew he was going to keep right on doing it.

'Proving a point,' he murmured, and he backed her into the corner of the lift.

'What…what point?'

'That you enjoyed our kiss as much as I did.'

'I— You—' She snapped her mouth closed.

'Admit it, and I won't kiss you again,' he whispered.

Her gaze collided with his. A strangled and indecipherable sound emerged from the back of her throat.

She couldn't do it.

She couldn't look him in the eye and lie.

It just wasn't in her nature.

Triumph raced through his system, arousing everything in its path.

Shara didn't know what to think—or feel.

The glitter in Royce's chocolate-brown eyes was a clear message.

He wanted her.

The thought sent excitement racing up and down her spine.

So too did the sheer male smell of him.

His eyes were on her mouth.

Every nerve-ending tingled in anticipation. Each muscle was straining—not away from him, but *towards* him.

Somehow their bodies must have recognised the deepening sexual tension in the confined space. Without either of them seeming to move the gap between them was demolished. Her soft curves were plastered against the hardness of his.

Their mouths came together with a sizzle, lips moving

hungrily as they matched kiss for aching kiss. Royce hauled her to the tips of her toes as his lips prised hers open. His tongue darted into the warm depths of her mouth.

Shara felt her legs buckle beneath her. If it weren't for the arms supporting her she would have fallen.

Shara pressed herself against him. The action squashed her aching breasts against the hardness of his chest. Winding her arms around his neck, she buried her fingers in the thick crispness of his hair, moaning as she felt his tongue delve into her mouth again.

Suddenly Royce lifted his head.

Shara wanted to drag his mouth back to hers, but she heard what Royce had obviously heard because his head was cocked to one side.

'Are you OK in there?' a male voice called.

Were they OK?

Shara couldn't answer for Royce, but for her part she was very far from being OK.

Her breathing was rushed and shallow, her breasts heavy, and there was a moist dampness at the juncture of her thighs that signalled just how far-reaching an effect he'd had on her.

Royce, who had been staring upwards, dropped his gaze to hers.

His face was expressionless.

He dropped his arms to his sides and stepped away from her.

Then he called out. 'We're fine. I accidentally pressed the emergency stop button.'

'OK. We'll have you out shortly.'

'Well, it can't be too soon for me,' Shara muttered. 'I can't wait to get out of here.'

She needed fresh air.

And distance.

Lots and lots of distance between her and Royce.

She also needed a brain transplant.

Or maybe a libido transplant.

She wasn't quite sure which.

All she knew was that as soon as his mouth had claimed hers her resolve not to respond had disappeared in a puff of smoke.

The lift jerked and then began moving. More slowly than it usually did. At a snail's pace.

Shara moved to stand in front of the doors.

Royce grabbed her arm and spun her to face him.

'Let me go.' Her voice sliced at him, and she yanked away her arm, which tingled where he'd touched.

Royce did as she asked. 'Before we leave this lift I want one thing clear,' he said, in a deep, firm voice.

Shara didn't respond. Knowing Royce, he'd say what was on his mind whether she prompted him or not.

'This ends right here.'

'This…?'

'This attraction between us. There will be no more kissing.'

Whatever she'd expected him to say, it wasn't that. She didn't know whether to be relieved or disappointed by his response. Her ambivalence annoyed her.

Even that was an understatement.

She was angry.

At herself—and Royce.

She tossed her head, jutted her chin, and slammed her hands down on her hips. 'You bet it won't. I don't know what you were thinking and I don't care. After what Steve has put me through the last thing I need is the hired help coming on to me. Got it?'

Royce froze.

He was angry.

More angry than he had a right to be.

Not just at Shara for her comment about him being the hired help—although he was disappointed by the remark.

He was angry at himself.

For creating this situation.

And he *had* created it.

He was the one who had grabbed Shara.

He was the one who had kissed her.

He was normally very much in control.

But he was beginning to sense—with the sensitivity of a jackhammer against concrete!—that his reactions to Shara were far from usual.

Kissing her had been the start of the lunacy.

Kissing her for a second time and pressing the emergency stop button had taken the madness a step further.

'Thank you for the timely reminder. I'm here to protect you. Nothing else. Let's keep it that way.'

Royce kept to his word.

Shara should have been pleased, but she wasn't.

Instead, she felt strangely disappointed. She also felt uncomfortable. She vacillated between wanting to apologise to him and then berating herself for feeling sorry for him.

It went on like that for two days.

By the end of the second day Shara had had enough.

She flung the magazine she'd been trying to read without any success down on to the sofa beside her and stomped into the kitchen, where Royce worked on his laptop and mobile phone every day.

'OK. Do you want me to apologise?' she demanded, stopping just inside the kitchen door and jamming her hands down on her hips.

Royce looked up slowly from his laptop and leaned back in his chair.

He really was the most handsome man. Every time she looked at him he took her breath away.

'Apologise for what?'

'For calling you the hired help,' she said.

Royce shrugged. 'That's entirely up to you.'

'But you don't care one way or another?'

'No. I don't.'

Shara stared at him. 'Well, whether you care or not, I'm sorry. I should never have made the comment. It was wrong. I lashed out without thinking.'

Having said what she'd come to say, she turned to leave. She was at the door when he said her name quietly behind her.

Slowly she turned to face him. 'What?'

'Thank you for the apology.'

She inclined her head. 'You're welcome. As I said, I should never have made the remark in the first place. As my old nanny used to say, "We all have to put our undies on the same way."'

Royce stared at her, then flung his head back and burst out laughing. When he finally calmed down he asked, 'Your old nanny said that?'

Shara could hardly speak. Royce looked twice as handsome as he usually did when he laughed like that. 'She did. She was a blunt and down-to-earth woman. It was her way of teaching me that everyone is equal.'

Royce nodded. 'So that's where you get it from.'

Shara frowned. 'Get what from?'

'Your frankness. If you haven't noticed, you're pretty direct yourself.'

Shara shrugged. 'Mrs P was with me for six years. I wouldn't be surprised if some of her attitude rubbed off on me.'

When Royce didn't say anything else Shara turned to leave again. This time she didn't even reach the door before Royce stopped her.

'Before you go, there's something we need to discuss.'

Again she turned slowly, and again her heart went berserk.

'What is it?' she asked, sounding so breathless she was barely able to recognise her own voice.

'We have a court date for the AVO.'

The air hissed from her lungs. For a minute—just one—she'd thought Royce was going to discuss their kiss with her. She didn't know whether to be relieved or disappointed that he hadn't.

'When?' she asked.

'Two weeks today.'

Shara absorbed the information. She'd expected the news to make her feel anxious, but it didn't. She was a little nervous, which was perfectly understandable, but that was about it. 'OK.'

'I think that will send a clear message to Brady. Hopefully he'll back off.'

That could well be the beginning of the end.

She greeted the thought with mixed feelings.

Obviously she was ecstatic at the thought of bringing Steve's campaign of terror to an end. But it also meant that Royce would walk out of her life.

That was a *good* thing, she assured herself.

So why then was there a distinct pang in the middle of her chest?

'Let's hope so.' She hesitated in the doorway. Waved a hand at the files and laptop. 'Do you have time for another karate lesson? Or are you too busy?'

Royce stared at her.

Shara laughed and waved another hand through the air. 'Forget it. It's a bad idea. I shouldn't have said anything. I need a break, that's all. I'll read a book or something.'

'How are the donations going for the ball?'

'I've called all the companies who donated something last year. I've left messages for some of them, but almost everyone I've spoken to is going to donate again.'

Royce whistled through his teeth. 'That must have taken some doing.'

She smiled. 'I had to twist an arm or two, but most of them were happy to help out.' She waved another hand. 'I'll get out of your hair now.'

Royce didn't respond. He just kept on staring at her with chocolate-brown eyes.

She didn't need to explain why a karate session was a bad idea. After the kiss they'd shared in the lift they both knew that they'd be inviting disaster.

She turned to leave for a third time. Had actually taken two steps into the hallway when he said her name again.

'What?' she asked over her shoulder.

'I could do with a break too,' he said slowly. 'Go and get changed. We'll meet in the lounge room in five minutes.'

'What are you *doing*?' Royce muttered to himself under his breath as he walked into the lounge room at the allotted time.

This was foolhardy at best, and at worst complete insanity.

Shara was waiting for him, dressed as she usually was in the almost see-through white cotton pants and a figure-hugging T-shirt that outlined the generous swell of her breasts and enough cleavage to make his body harden.

'OK. Where do we start?' she asked.

Royce took a seat on the sofa. 'I'd like you to demonstrate what you've learned so far.'

There was only one way he was going to survive this session, and that was by adopting a hands-free approach.

'Come on,' he said. 'Let's see what you remember.'

Shara got into the first starting position and one by one went through the various blocks, punches and kicks he'd taught her.

Royce tried to concentrate on her technique.

But more and more he found his focus drifting to other things.

Like how serious she looked as she concentrated on doing each movement to the best of her ability. The frown creasing her forehead and the little moue she made with her lips.

And of course the other huge distraction was her body.

Her muscles flexed and released. Her belly contracted. So, too, did her buttocks.

And then there were her breasts. They jiggled ever so slightly with every movement. And every jiggle made his body harden more and more, until he was ready to jump to his feet and—

No!

Don't even think about it.

If he did he was likely to become undone.

But, try as he might, he couldn't control where he looked or how he felt.

Shara was almost at the end of her demonstration when the phone rang. Her arms immediately dropped to her sides, her expression growing tense.

Royce clenched his teeth. His patience was growing thin at Brady's daily dose of terror.

Reaching out, he pulled the plug from the wall socket.

'Continue,' he said, waving a hand.

'You can't do that.'

'Of course I can. If it's important they'll call you on your mobile.'

What he meant, of course, was that if it was anyone other than Brady they would call her on her mobile.

Shara picked up where she'd left off. When she'd finished, she asked, 'What next?'

If he had any sense he'd end the session then and there. Instead, he rose to his feet. His heart was pounding. 'You're ready to do some very basic sparring. I want you to attack me. Hit, kick, punch. Whatever you like. I'll block you and make an attacking movement of my own. Then we'll try it in reverse.'

'OK.' Shara aimed a punch at his belly. Royce blocked, dipped, and then aimed an answering punch gently to the side of her head.

This time she kicked and then punched him. Royce blocked both moves, spun around, and aimed a kick at her knee.

After about ten minutes Royce said, 'OK, your turn. This time I'm going to attack you. I want you to concentrate on defending yourself.'

Shara raised her hands in defensive mode.

As quick as a flash Royce made a soft chop to the side of her neck. 'Hey, that was too easy.'

'I wasn't ready,' Shara protested.

Royce moved more slowly this time, aiming a fist at her solar plexus. Shara blocked him with a throw of her left arm, then moved into a punch.

Royce blocked her effortlessly. 'Well, well, well. You're full of surprises, aren't you?'

She grinned. 'You bet.'

Royce backed off a pace to see what Shara would do.

They danced around on their toes, hands raised in fighting position. Shara aimed a punch towards Royce's chest. He blocked it with a swing of his left arm.

Royce moved to the left, feinted, quickly put his left foot behind her right ankle and pushed. Surprise and momentum sent Shara tumbling to the floor.

Royce followed her down, pinning her to the rug with his weight.

The feel of her beneath him sent a shimmering wave of heat through his entire body. The cushioning fullness of her breasts and the welcoming dip of her hips sent his blood pressure skyrocketing.

Royce took both of her hands in his and pinned them to

the carpet on either side of her head. He'd never thought of karate as foreplay, but that was exactly what it felt like.

Excitement had been building from the moment Shara had suggested the session.

In the last ten minutes it had gone right off the charts.

Breaking point had come and gone in the blink of an eye.

Royce didn't think twice. He didn't think at all. He simply bent his head and crushed her mouth with his.

Shara kissed him straight back.

Excitement rushed through him. So potent it made his blood fizz and stretched every inch of his skin.

In an action as ancient as time Royce pressed his erection against her. Shara moaned and tugged her hands free. Her arms wrapped around his neck, her fingers weaving into his hair.

Royce trailed his mouth over the delicate arch of her cheekbone to her earlobe, where he sucked on the sensitive flesh.

Shara's body moved restlessly beneath his.

From her ear, his mouth moved lower, trailing a path of liquid fire down her throat. He paused at its base, his tongue flicking against her frantically beating pulse, before moving lower still.

He buried his face between her breasts and inhaled her scent. It circulated in his bloodstream like heady wine.

'Yes,' Shara muttered, her hands clutching at his shoulders, her nails digging into his flesh.

Royce ran his hands over her bone-melting curves, undecided on which part to linger, trying to enjoy each delectable inch of her all at once.

He raised his head and stared down at her.

Her eyelids lifted slowly, as if they were heavy. The fire he saw in her eyes echoed deep inside of him.

'You're wearing too many clothes,' he said, in a voice he hardly recognised as his own.

Shara nodded, as if she were incapable of speech.

With the aid of her wriggling, Royce pulled her T-shirt
up over her head. He stared down at what he'd revealed: ripe
breasts spilling out of the cups of her bra.

His loins kicked, and then kicked again even harder.

His blood pulsed so strongly he could feel it beating against
the underside of his skin.

'Do you know how long I've wanted to see you like this?'
he asked, the question dragged from deep inside him.

Shara shook her head.

'For ever,' he whispered.

It was the most incongruous answer. It didn't make sense.
And yet on a primitive level, where DNA met energy and
created life, it was true. True in a way that he couldn't even
begin to understand.

Sliding a hand beneath her back, he unfastened her bra
and slowly stripped it away.

His breath caught in the back of his throat

Slowly he raised his hands. For several moments they hov-
ered in the air, and then he cupped a breast in each hand. As
he'd thought more than once, she fitted him perfectly. As if
she'd been made just for him. The pads of his thumbs rubbed
across her nipples, which immediately sprang erect.

Shara moaned and arched her back, pressing against him.

He played with her breasts for a few more moments before dropping his head and drawing one hard bead into his
mouth, rolling it with his tongue.

Shara thrashed her head from side to side, a keening cry
that sounded half-pleasure, half-protest coming from the back
of her throat.

And then she moved.

Her clutching hands left his shoulders and ran down over
the hard planes of his back, exploring as she went. She tugged
on the hem of his T-shirt. Lifting his head, Royce helped strip
it away.

His hands immediately went to the waistband of her white

trousers. He didn't linger over their removal. He was too aroused to take things slowly.

His pants quickly followed.

When one of her hands insinuated itself between their tightly pressed bodies Royce knew exactly what was coming. Still, nothing could prepare him for the first delicate touch of her fingers on his erection.

When her hand closed around him, Royce froze. So much pulsating energy rushed to where she touched that he shuddered. When her hand moved he shuddered again.

'Enough,' he growled, barely able to get the word out as he clasped her wrist and pulled her hand away from him.

He was so aroused he was shaking.

A line from an old tune popped into his head.

There's a fine line between pleasure and pain.

He was on the border of that line right now.

He'd never visited this particular place before.

Never felt the way he felt right now.

CHAPTER SEVEN

WHEN a hand settled hotly between her legs, Shara felt a rush of heat that shook her to the very foundations of her being. Clutching at Royce's powerful back with claw-like fingers, she gasped as his fingers delicately probed the centre of her heat, his lingering caress driving her wild with anticipation. When his hand danced a rhythmic tattoo on the nub of her desire Shara felt as if she was about to shatter into a million pieces.

As if realising how close she was to coming, Royce used his free hand to caress her slowly, as though trying to soothe the flames his other hand had ignited.

It didn't help.

She was beyond help.

She couldn't take much more. She was at the very brink of a throbbing abyss. Royce kept her on the very edge, as if he enjoyed torturing her.

His fingers left her and were replaced by the probing hardness of his erection. Shara circled his waist with her legs, hooking her ankles together to hold him captive against her. She rotated her hips, urging him to enter her and end the suspense, the torture.

As she moved against him Royce moaned, but still he didn't give her what she so desperately wanted.

Lifting her head, Shara nipped at his bottom lip with her teeth.

'Now. Please now,' she begged brokenly.

As if her plea was exactly what he'd been waiting for, Royce thrust inside her.

They moaned in unison.

For several long moments neither of them moved. Shara could have stayed that way for ever, enjoying the silken hardness of him filling and stretching her.

And then there was no more thought as Royce started to move within her, a slow rhythm at first, then faster. Shara moved with him, matching thrust for nerve-quivering thrust, tightening her legs around his waist and pulling him deeper and deeper.

The tension built, spiralled, and threw her sky-high.

In the next instant the world exploded into a mass of sheer sensation. A pulsating throb started deep in her womb and extended outwards until every bit of her was consumed by it. Her internal muscles clenched around him, her fingers clawing at his back.

Royce gave one final thrust, finding his own release with a muttered cry.

Shara's limbs felt heavy and molten. Royce shuddered against her.

The wild beat of his heart matched the hammer of hers.

What they had just shared had been the most incredible experience of her life.

But as her heartbeat slowly returned to normal Shara plummeted back to earth with a bang.

Her mind was filled with visions of what had just happened.

Of hands and mouths, touching and tasting.

Everywhere.

She wished the memories would disappear, but they were indelibly imprinted on her memory banks.

Even in the good times with Steve sex had never been so intense or exciting. The passion that had sheared through her with Royce had turned her inside out.

The fact that it had been so intense disturbed her.

A frisson of…

Of what…?

Anxiety? Panic?

She wasn't sure what.

A frisson of *something* rippled through her like a gust of cold wind.

'I can't do this,' she said, pushing against Royce's shoulders. 'I'm sorry. I just can't do this.'

Royce heeded her urging and rolled on to his back.

Shara scrambled to her feet and snatched up her clothes. Hugging them to her chest, she glanced at Royce to see if he was watching her.

He wasn't.

His eyes were closed.

Quickly she pulled on her clothes to cover her nakedness.

When she was done she remained standing where she was, not sure what to do. She wanted to run out of the room and go somewhere. Anywhere. As long as it was away from Royce.

But that smacked of running away. Given her resolve to stand up for herself, she didn't particularly want to take the cowardly way out.

Her eyes roamed his naked figure. She wished the action left her immune but was very much aware that it didn't.

When she got to his face she was disconcerted to find that his eyes were open and he was watching her. Embarrassed heat flooded her cheeks and made the tips of her ears burn.

He moved to get up.

Shara turned her back on him.

She heard the rustle of clothing. She imagined him putting on his trousers and shirt. Imagined the ripple of muscle and the scent of warm male skin as he did so.

The images were so vivid that Shara scrunched up her eyes, but it didn't help.

'You can turn around now,' Royce said dryly.

If anything the heat in her cheeks burned even more hotly. Slowly—reluctantly—she turned to face him.

'Let's get straight to the point, shall we?' Royce spoke as calmly as if he were discussing the weather or the price of a loaf of bread. 'What just happened shouldn't have happened. Right?'

Relief poured through her. So too did an entirely unexpected pang of disappointment.

Hands clasped tightly together in front of her, Shara nodded. 'No. I mean yes. It shouldn't have happened. I just don't want to get involved again. I…I don't think I can handle it.'

It wasn't just about sex.

It was about the exchange of power.

With men it was always a one way street—with the woman on the losing end.

Well, she'd been there, done that. She wasn't going there again.

Straightening her spine and squaring her shoulders, Shara stared him straight in the eye.

Royce nodded.

Her heart plummeted to her toes and stayed there.

There was a sinking sensation in the pit of her stomach.

Both were quite patently ridiculous reactions.

She wasn't disappointed by his agreement. She wasn't.

This was what she wanted.

Wasn't it?

'I understand,' Royce said with another nod.

He sounded calm and in control, but inside he was a seething mass of emotions.

He didn't understand it.

He should be applauding.

Shara was saying everything he wanted to hear.

She wasn't clinging.

She wasn't trying to turn the situation to her advantage.

So why was he so displeased with her response?

Royce wasn't sure, and that made him even more displeased.

He was an analytical kind of guy.

Logical.

He knew that one plus one equalled two—not twenty.

So why did nothing about this situation make sense?

He knew that getting involved with Shara was wrong—and not just because he couldn't afford a distraction on the job.

It was more than that.

Alarm bells had started ringing almost from the beginning.

There was something about Shara that had got under his skin from day one.

Her hoity-toity tone had got his back up when normally such an attitude would have bounced straight off him.

His reaction to what she'd endured at the hands of Brady had been...

Well, it had been *emotional*, damn it!

Not professional. Not detached. Not anything it should have been.

It was as if his sympathy for her had sucked him over a line he hadn't crossed since the day he'd learned the truth about Fiona—and that was more than enough to make him wary.

'Good,' Shara said.

Her voice sounded flat.

Royce searched her face.

Did she feel the same way he did? That what they'd shared had blown his mind and just about everything else?

No, he had to forget about that or he was a goner. He had to concentrate on the reasons they shouldn't get involved.

'You've just gone through a marriage break up. You're being stalked by your ex-husband. The last thing you need is another man in your life,' he said, repeating her words back at her. 'That makes perfect sense. I completely understand.'

Shara was nodding. 'That's right. I don't.'

'And I'm here to do a job,' Royce said. 'I can't do that properly if I get involved. I need to stay objective.'

'Of course you do,' she said. 'This makes no sense for either of us.'

She was being helpful.

And co-operative.

But he wanted neither of those things.

It didn't matter how many 't's he crossed or how many 'i's he dotted, he wanted her. It went against every rational thought he possessed but that didn't change anything.

Thankfully, before he did anything stupid, like kiss her again, his mobile phone started ringing. Extracting the phone from his pocket, he glanced at the screen and frowned.

He looked up. 'I'm sorry but I'm going to have to take this. It's the Los Angeles office.'

Shara inclined her head, her face expressionless. 'No problem. We've said all we needed to say.'

As Royce watched her walk out of the room he couldn't help feeling she was wrong about that.

What was he going to do?

Royce rubbed his jaw.

Damn. What was the matter with him? The answer was simple. He had to bring in one of his people to finish this job while he concentrated on the high-profile case he'd just received.

Gerard Atwood would understand, he was sure. There were a number of points in his favour.

One, the AVO was in place and would no doubt be upheld by the courts in a fortnight's time.

And, two, he only hired the best people. Shara would be more than safe with any of his operatives.

He just had to figure out who he could use.

That new girl Kelly Walker had impressed him with her work so far. He'd even been thinking of giving her a promotion.

He frowned.

But, no, Kelly was working the Reynolds case.

Bob Brisket, then. If his memory served him correctly Bob was the only operative available at the moment. But even as the idea formed Royce dismissed it. Bob wasn't the right person. He was a good investigator, but too abrasive for bodyguard duty.

Well, there had to be a solution.

He snapped his fingers in the air and smiled. He had it. His friend Travis Knight could help him. Travis had worked with him before. He knew the ropes. In fact, Travis was one of the best—despite the fact that he preferred trading on the stockmarket for a living.

Picking up his mobile, Royce rapidly punched in the number.

'Travis, old buddy. Long time no speak,' Royce said when Travis finally picked up the phone.

'Royce, where have you been? I was beginning to think you'd fallen off the face of the earth.'

'Not quite.' Royce laughed. 'I've been busy, as usual. What about you? Still playing around with that computer of yours?'

'I'll have you know I work very hard on that computer of mine,' Travis replied, mock-indignantly.

'Sure,' Royce joked. 'For all of three hours a day.'

'Sometimes I push myself and make it four,' Travis joked in return. 'How's business with you?'

'Fine. Fine. Couldn't be better,' Royce murmured quietly. 'But I'm in a bit of a bind at the moment. I need to ask you a favour.'

'Done,' Travis replied promptly. 'You name it.'

'Do you mean that?'

'Of course I do. Do you really think I'm likely to say no? You, Jackson and I may not be the Three Musketeers, but we come damn close. One for all and all for one. You know that.'

Royce did know. Which was precisely why he didn't want to take advantage of Travis.

'Thanks. I'm involved in a case at the moment and the Los Angeles office has just booked me in to protect a visiting celebrity without bothering to check my schedule,' Royce said with frustration. 'Not that I want to miss out on this one. It's high-profile and comes with a fantastic fee. That's why I need you to take on the assignment.'

As soon as the words were out of his mouth Royce stopped, hardly able to believe what he'd just said.

Had he really just asked Travis to take over the Taylor Zane case?

Royce replayed his words back in his head.

Yes, that was exactly what he'd said.

It was the exact opposite of what he'd intended to ask, which was for Travis to look after Shara while *he* took care of Taylor Zane.

How had that happened?

Royce wasn't really sure, and really didn't care.

Because the minute he'd said them the words had felt right.

Although it sounded ridiculous even to his own ears, he didn't trust anyone else to protect Shara.

He shook his head. He must be going crazy.

Travis obviously thought so too, because he said, very doubtfully, 'Royce, I haven't done anything like that for a while. Surely you have someone else on your team who could take over?'

'Not for this particular client. I need someone I can really trust. And that's you,' Royce answered emphatically. 'I'd do it myself, except I'm needed here.'

And he *was* needed here. The almost daily phone calls from Brady were proof of that. So too was that brief glimpse he'd had of what he was sure was the other man in disguise.

Gut instinct was telling him to stay on Shara's case. And if there was one thing he'd learned it was to listen to his instincts.

Staying on the case had nothing to do with the incredible sex they'd shared.

He was just doing his job.

Shara stayed in her room for the rest of the day.

She tried to pretend she wasn't hiding, but the way she tensed every time she heard a noise somewhere in the house forced her to admit that that was exactly what she was doing.

Rightly or wrongly, she didn't want to face Royce.

They'd had sex in the middle of her father's expensive Aubusson rug, for goodness' sake.

Mind-blowing, nerve-twisting, gut-wrenching sex.

Sex that had been so explosive it had torn her entire thought processes to shreds.

How could she have done something so stupid?

It was another poor decision in the long line of poor decisions she just seemed to keep on making.

Another snake's head she'd jumped on all by herself.

Finally hunger drove her from her bedroom in search of food.

Slipping a peach-coloured bathrobe over the top of her nightdress, she carefully opened her door, trying to make as little noise as possible.

The last thing she wanted to do was wake Royce.

She wasn't ready to face him yet.

She was too scared.

Scared...?

The word made Shara stop dead in her tracks halfway down the stairs.

She wasn't scared.

Was she…?

The breath caught in her throat and her heart did a strange *kerthump* in her chest. The question cut through the web of chaotic thoughts that had besieged her since she'd taken refuge in her room.

Yes, she was scared.

But she wasn't scared of Royce.

She was scared of herself.

Afraid of how she'd react.

Because there was one fact she couldn't escape.

Regardless of why she shouldn't get involved with Royce, she already was—whether she wanted to be or not.

Royce was lying on his back with his arms folded beneath his head, staring at the ceiling, when he heard the creak of a floorboard. Almost simultaneously his laptop began beeping, indicating movement in the house.

Either they had an intruder, or Shara was up and about.

Given that none of the downstairs motion detectors had gone off, Royce could only presume it was Shara.

Which left him with a decision to make.

Stay where he was…or get up and follow her.

Royce knew exactly what he should do.

Stay in bed.

It wasn't as if Shara could go anywhere without him knowing about it. The household security system would alert him if she tried to leave the house—although where she would go in the middle of the night he didn't have a clue.

So he should stay in bed where it was safe.

Safe…?

The word made Royce jack-knife into a sitting position, his body growing rigid, muscles locking.

Safety played a large part in his life. The security business could be rough, and it could be tough. He'd been in dangerous situations, life-threatening situations, more than once and no doubt would be again.

But did he really see Shara as dangerous?

Beautiful? Yes.

Sexy? Yes.

But *dangerous*…?

The breath locked tight in his lungs, and his heart did a massive leap in his chest as the answer seared into his brain.

Yes, Shara was dangerous.

She was getting under his skin.

Making him think things he didn't want to think.

Making him *do* things he didn't want to do.

Like making love to her in the middle of her father's Aubusson rug.

Like making him turn over Taylor Zane's case to Travis so that he could stay and protect her.

Like making him follow her in the middle of the night when he should really stay in bed.

Because, whether it made sense or not, that was exactly what he was going to do.

He couldn't explain it. He didn't even begin to try.

He simply dragged in a breath, swung his legs over the edge of the bed and rose to his feet.

Then, pulling on a pair of worn denims, he went after her.

A sound in the doorway made Shara jump ten feet in the air. Her heart pounded, her hand going to the base of her throat.

She looked towards the source of the sound—and froze.

Royce was lounging in the doorway, watching her.

Her heart stopped and then kick-started again. Her mouth was parchment-dry. A slow burn started deep in her belly.

He looked absolutely mouthwateringly gorgeous. Like a sexy advertisement for denim jeans.

Because that was all he was wearing.

His jeans had obviously been slung on in a hurry. They

sat low on his hips, the zip only half done up and the button hanging open.

His chest was broad and deep, the skin smooth and golden-brown. Her eyes drifted lower to the rippling display of muscle on his belly before dropping lower still, to the tantalisingly undone button and the zipper just beneath.

A deep shuddering breath escaped her constricted throat as her eyes travelled back upwards.

His hair was tousled and the shadow of a beard was beginning to darken his strong, square jaw.

Her eyes met his.

Desire sizzled along her nerve-endings.

He was looking at her as if…

As if…

As if he wanted to strip her naked and take her where she was standing!

The knife she was holding clattered to the benchtop. 'Don't sneak up on me like that,' she said, dragging her eyes away from him.

'I didn't sneak. I walked.' He levered himself away from the doorjamb and walked further into the room.

Shara couldn't look away, her eyes captured by the ripple of his muscles as he walked.

'You obviously didn't hear me.'

Shara wasn't surprised. She'd been deep in thought. Not about the sandwich she was making. Not about whether to have mustard or pickle.

No, she'd been thinking about that taboo subject.

Royce.

And then suddenly he was here, as if her thinking about him had somehow conjured him up.

Swallowing, she picked up the knife and gestured to the sandwich. 'Are you hungry?'

'Yes.'

Her eyes shot to his face. There was something in the way

he'd said that one word and something in the glitter of his eyes that suggested they weren't just talking about food.

Her already frantically beating heart took off at a gallop. She licked her lips. 'I meant do you want a sandwich?'

'No.'

His monosyllabic answer sent hormones hurtling through her system, setting off one vibration after another against her nerve-endings.

'Then what *do* you want?'

The words burst out of her mouth at the exact same time the thought popped into her head. She hadn't meant to say them out loud. She would have stopped them if she could, but it was too late.

It was still a good question.

Because she couldn't shake the feeling that their conversation was operating on two levels.

Royce stared at her without speaking. His eyes were still glittering, and the angles and planes of his face seemed to be standing out more sharply.

Shara swallowed. And swallowed again.

She dropped the knife for a second time and wrapped her arms around herself. 'I mean why are you here?'

There was any number of answers Royce could give to that question.

He was hungry. Or he couldn't sleep. Or he'd come downstairs for a book.

But Shara hoped it was none of those things.

Rightly or wrongly, she hoped that he'd heard her come downstairs and had followed her.

It was a damned good question.

In fact both of them were.

It wasn't the first time Shara had put him on the spot.

She seemed to be making quite a habit out of it.

And each time the questions made the truth jump up and smack him in the face.

Because, if only to himself, he had to answer them honestly.

Question: What do you want?

Answer: You.

Question: Why are you here?

Answer: You.

That was why he'd got out of bed and followed her.

That was why he was standing here like a dumb jerk, with his insides so twisted in knots he could hardly think straight.

Royce wasn't sure when he'd decided he was going to make love to her again.

Had it been a split-second decision made when he'd heard the creaking floorboard? Or had he made it when he'd walked into the room and seen Shara standing there looking so beautiful?

Or was it the fact that *she* was asking the difficult questions while he was hiding from the truth?

And he *was* hiding from the truth.

Because the truth was that he wanted her.

'This is why I'm here,' he said, and reached across the distance separating them and hauled her into his arms.

Shara leapt into the kiss with a hunger that left her shaking inside.

How could she want Royce so much?

So much that she *ached* for him?

She didn't know and didn't care.

By the time Royce lifted his head they were both breathing heavily.

They stared at each other, dark eyes locked with blue. They didn't talk. They barely seemed to be breathing. As if the slightest movement might break the spell that bound them together.

Neither did they touch each other—unless you counted the hard points of her breasts whispering feather-like against his sleekly muscled chest through the thin fabric of her nightgown and robe.

The look in his eyes was incredible. So hot that it created a fire inside of her.

Royce ran a finger down her cheek to the corner of her mouth, which was tingling from his kisses. 'That's why I followed you. I want to make love to you again.'

Her breath hitched. 'What about not mixing business with pleasure?'

Royce shrugged. 'I'm the boss. If anyone can bend the rules it's me. You have to decide whether this is what you want or not.'

Shara dragged in a deep breath. And then another.

Her eyes landed on his mouth and a quiver of longing ran through her.

The cowardly part of her wished that Royce had just kept right on kissing her. It would have been easier if he'd swept her away into a maelstrom of passion.

But his words wouldn't let her do that.

They confronted her.

Forced her to make a choice.

It should be an easy one.

Step back. Say no. Put an end to all this nonsense.

But somehow she just couldn't do it.

Couldn't do it because she didn't *want* to do it.

What she wanted was Royce.

The realisation made the air lock tight in her lungs.

It was no use pretending any more.

No use trying to ignore what was impossible to ignore.

She wanted the guy.

She wanted the guy more than she'd ever wanted Steve.

More than she'd ever dreamed was possible.

Her heart turned over as she lifted her eyes to his. 'I want you.'

A flash of triumph crossed his face. Shara didn't care. All it proved was that he wanted her as much as she wanted him.

'Are you sure?' he asked.

Shara nodded. 'I'm sure.'

And, strangely, given her record for making poor decisions, she *was* sure.

Even before she'd finished speaking Royce had swept her up against him, his mouth crashing down on hers.

With their mouths still fused Royce pushed her robe off her shoulders. It dropped unnoticed to the floor.

His hands immediately went to her nightdress, which he tugged up to her waist, then over the obstacle of her breasts. Their mouths disconnected only long enough for him to reef it over her head and toss it over his shoulder.

Shara writhed against him as his hands cupped her breasts.

Her fingers went to the zipper of his jeans. As she pulled it the rest of the way down her fingers brushed against his straining erection. His body shook and shuddered.

His hands made long sweeping movements over her body. Skimming some parts and lingering in others. When his fingers probed the moistness between her silken thighs she cried out loud, her nails clawing at his shoulders.

He was watching her with such a molten look in his eyes that her knees buckled. She would have fallen if he hadn't acted quickly. He caught her with one strong arm. The other made a sweeping motion across the kitchen bench.

Once he'd cleared a space he lifted her on to the edge of the bench and moved between her spread thighs.

'Please,' she begged. 'I want you.'

She hooked her legs around his hips and urged him towards her, needing him to hurry.

And then he was inside her, filling her with silken heat,

and she shuddered, clenching her muscles against the hard fullness of him.

'Look at me,' Royce commanded softly.

Shara opened heavy lids and locked her gaze with his. She couldn't look away as he started to move inside her, setting up a primitive rhythm she was powerless to deny.

And still they looked at each other. As inner tension built to an exquisite crescendo their eyes clung to each other as surely as their bodies did.

There was no more thought, just feeling. Their lovemaking was hard and fast, the sheer force of their passion cocooning them in a world of pure sensation. So intensely did Shara feel each stroke inside her body that it was exquisite torture. Torture she wanted to end, and at the same time wanted to continue for ever.

When the final pleasure crashed upon them in waves she cried out. From the sound of his own cry Royce found his own climax seconds later.

Shara collapsed against him. Royce closed his arms around her and buried his face in the curve of her neck. They stayed that way, panting, for several long moments.

Finally Royce lifted his head, a rueful smile lifting the corners of his mouth. 'First the lounge room and now the kitchen. Do you think we're ever going to make it to a bed?'

Shara burst out laughing, a blush heating her cheeks. Then she stroked her hands down over the hard planes of his back. 'I sure hope so. Why don't we go and find one now?'

CHAPTER EIGHT

SHARA woke slowly, stretching her arms and legs. When she felt a warm, hard body behind her, she froze.

Memories of the night before flooded through her like a series of still photographs.

Royce standing in the kitchen doorway, wearing nothing but a pair of low-slung denim jeans.

Royce staring deep into her eyes and saying, 'This is why I'm here,' just before pulling her into his arms and kissing her.

She rolled on to her side and found Royce leaning up on one elbow, staring down at her. His hair was mussed, a sexy stubble darkening his jaw.

'Good morning,' he said, a small smile lifting the corners of his mouth.

'Good morning,' she said, trying to smile back but not quite managing it.

He obviously sensed that she wasn't entirely comfortable with the situation, because he reached out and stroked a hand down her hair. 'Any regrets?'

She thought about that for a moment. 'Regret is the wrong word.'

'Then what is the right word?'

She searched her mind, trying to put a label on what she was feeling. 'I'm not sure. Concerned. Uncertain. Anxious.'

They were both talking quietly. Shara wasn't sure why. It wasn't as if anyone could overhear them. But somehow their hushed tones seemed appropriate.

Royce was no longer smiling, his chocolate brown eyes serious. 'Because of Brady?

'Partly.' Suddenly lying facing Royce no longer seemed right. She shuffled up on to the pillow, clutching the sheet to her breast, and stared straight ahead.

Royce pushed himself into a sitting position and swivelled to face her. 'Tell me what you're thinking.'

Shara pleated the sheet with her fingers, a knot in her stomach and a lump in her throat. 'I don't know how to explain it. All I know is that whatever else relationships are all about they are also about the balance of power. Women usually end up on the losing end of that equation.'

'Not always.'

She shrugged, staring at her fingers as they worked the cotton fabric into a concertina and then smoothed it back out again. 'Perhaps. But in my experience they are.' She turned and gave Royce a fierce look. 'I'm *never* going to hand power over to a man again. I'm *never* going to lose sight of myself again.'

Royce didn't rush to answer her. Finally he said softly, 'I'm not Brady. I'm not even remotely like Brady.'

'No, you're not. But you're a strong man. I'm not talking about physically. I'm talking about mentally. You're determined and stubborn and you like getting your own way.'

'I—'

She held up a hand. 'Don't deny it. You told me so yourself. You said that you'd handle this situation *your* way. That's the only way you do business. You have to have full control.'

He inclined his head. 'And I won't apologise for it. When it comes to the job—particularly when someone's safety's involved—it won't work any other way. I'm an expert. I'm trained in these situations. You're not. But that's the job. Outside of it—'

'Outside of it, what? You're different?'

'Yes, I *am* different. My parents brought me up to respect women. Their relationship is very much a partnership. In their marriage the balance of power you mentioned is well and truly equal. My mother wouldn't have it any other way.' He smiled. 'You'd like my mother. She is one of the most generous, warm-hearted people I know. But she's also one of the strongest.'

Shara wasn't quite sure what to say to that. 'I only have your word for that.'

'Yes, you do. Just as you only have my word for it that I will respect you while we're together and treat you as an equal.'

That was all he said.

He didn't try to persuade her.

Didn't try to sway her opinion in any way.

He just stared at her unwaveringly.

Shara stared into his chocolate-brown eyes.

She thought back over the last week or so.

She'd learned a lot about him in that relatively short period of time. But now, looking back, one thing struck her more deeply than anything else.

She'd recognised some time ago that Royce was different from the other men in her life, but it had only just dawned on her *how* different he was.

Royce was the first man—the *only* man—who had sought to empower her rather than dominate her.

It was as simple and yet as profound as that.

The knowledge rippled through her like a wave.

Royce had invested time and effort to teach her karate. To give her the skills and the confidence to fight back in a situation that until now had made her feel cowed and powerless.

He'd also encouraged her, supported her and listened to her.

'I believe you,' she said slowly.

'Good.' Royce drew her into his arms and brushed her mouth with his in a kiss so tender it made her want to weep. 'Let's just take one day at a time.'

'Yes,' she breathed, feeding her hands into the hair on either side of his head. 'Just one day at a time.'

'How did you break your nose?'

Royce rubbed the bump and laughed. 'Don't tell me you're still harking back to the movie version of what I do? I can assure you that I'm no James Bond.'

He was wrong about that.

He was very much like James Bond.

He was just as good-looking and he had the same kind of head-turning charisma. He was charming and capable and efficient, not to mention suave and sophisticated.

Had she mentioned good-looking?

Yes, she was sure she had.

He also possessed an I'm-sure-of-my-place-in-the-world and I-can-get-out-of-any-situation kind of confidence.

'So, how *did* you break your nose?' she asked again, determined not to let him put her off.

He laughed. 'I hate to disappoint you, Shara, but I broke my nose falling out of a tree when I was eight years old.'

'Oh.' She couldn't hide her disappointment.

He laughed again.

'You must have some interesting stories, though.' Shara refused to be thwarted. She found what he did for a living fascinating. 'What's the most bizarre case you've ever worked on?'

Royce rubbed the side of his jaw thoughtfully. Then his eyes lit up. 'That would have to be Zeus.'

If she remembered her history correctly, then Zeus was the king of all the other gods and the ruler of Mount Olympus. She was imagining a nasty crime boss similar to the Godfather when she prompted, 'Zeus?'

He nodded. 'Yes—Zeus the Chihuahua.'

Shara sputtered. 'A Chihuahua? You're pulling my leg!'

Royce shook his head, then made the sign of the cross. 'Cross my heart and hope to die. His owner, Mrs Pemberton, lives in New York. She was going on a Caribbean cruise with someone who was allergic to dogs. She hired me to doggy-guard Zeus while she was away.'

Shara searched his face. 'You're having me on?'

Royce shook his head. 'No—and get this: Zeus came complete with a dog collar made from a small fortune in diamonds. I never could figure out whether it was the dog she was worried about or the stones.'

'You're making this up. You have to be.'

'I'm afraid not. The lady has more money than sense. And damn but that dog is ugly.'

Shara laughed, as she was sure he'd intended.

She laughed a lot around Royce—and it felt good.

'So, tell me, what does the A stand for?' Shara asked.

Royce shook his head even as he gave a rueful laugh. 'Don't you ever give up?' he asked, referring to the fact that every day for the last week she'd asked the very same question.

'Nope,' she said, her blue eyes sparkling with mischief.

Daringly, she slid her hand under the sheet until her fingers closed around him, immediately feeling him swell beneath her touch.

He moaned and closed his eyes, his back arching ever so slightly.

'Are you sure you don't want to tell me?' she drawled, moving her hand slowly up and down.

'You witch,' he accused, swiftly rolling over and capturing her hand between their bodies. 'You shouldn't have done that!'

Shara let a small smile play about her mouth. 'I shouldn't?' she asked innocently.

Shaking his head, Royce laughed. 'No, you shouldn't. You won't get an answer now. I have other things on my mind.'

With a small tug under the sheets she prompted, '*Mind?* I thought it was another part of your anatomy that was paying attention.'

Shara loved the freedom she felt to touch Royce and tease him the way he did her. Loved the way his body responded so quickly every time she touched him, too.

With his chocolate-coloured eyes sinfully locked on her breasts, Royce gave a wicked grin. 'Oh, there's more than one part of my anatomy that's engaged at the moment. There are my eyes, which are absolutely captivated by your beautiful breasts.'

His hands lifted and palmed the weighty globes. Her skin leapt to his touch, her breasts peaking into tight nubs.

'And then of course there's my hands,' he muttered raggedly, dark eyes fixed on the way his hands were playing with her rock-hard nipples. 'They're very busy at the moment.'

The quicksilver flash of desire slid over every nerve-ending as she pressed her aching breasts into his hands.

'And you're wrong.' His voice was getting huskier by the minute. 'My mind is very much occupied. At the moment, it's busy thinking about what you look like when I enter you. The way your eyes widen at first and then close for a minute. And when they open again they're not a sparkling blue any more. They're a deep, dark purple.'

An inarticulate sound escaped her strangled throat. The combination of stroking hands and the tantalising picture his words evoked were turning her on so much she was shaking with it.

As if realising she had a desperate need to be kissed, Royce feathered the lightest of kisses across her mouth.

'No,' Shara protested as he moved away, lifting her arms up around his neck, trying to tug his head back down to hers. She wanted him to kiss her properly, to take her mouth in that hungry and possessive way he had.

She *needed* him to kiss her that way.

But he was stronger than she was, and he obviously had something else in mind, because his head dipped and he trailed a string of feather-light kisses down her throat and into the valley between her breasts.

Shara quivered under his delicate touch. But she needed more.

'Royce, please...'

Royce felt his body clench spasmodically as he heard Shara's moaned plea.

He looked into her face, seeing the wanting stamped there. Her cheeks were flushed, her eyes dilating. If he could capture on film or on canvass what she looked like when he made love to her he would. It wouldn't be a picture for public consumption. It would be for his eyes alone. He didn't want anyone else to know what she looked like when he pleasured her.

'Please what?' he asked, placing another delicate kiss on the slope of one breast.

An inarticulate sound escaped her throat.

'This?' he asked softly, as he lowered his head and flicked at one rose-pink nipple with the tip of his tongue.

'Yes,' she gasped, grabbing his head and pulling him back down to her.

His body clenched again—even harder.

The same line from that old tune popped into his head again.

There's a fine line between pleasure and pain.

Well, Royce was pretty damned sure he'd just crossed it.

With a groan he took one nipple fully into his mouth. As he did so, he trailed his fingers gently over the swell of her tummy.

She quivered.

Her response gave him a heady rush of pleasure. Never had giving a woman pleasure meant so much to him. Nor had he received so much in return.

She did things to him no other woman had managed to do.

He dipped a finger into her belly button as he explored the smooth, soft skin of her stomach. Slowly he trailed his fingers down until they slipped between her thighs. He just let his hand rest there. Temptingly. Tauntingly. Enough to make her arch her pelvis up towards his waiting hand.

'You're so hot,' he whispered against her breast. Delicately, he probed her moistness with his fingers, moaning out loud when he felt how wet and ready she was for him. His body jerked as he was struck by a wave of such powerful desire he couldn't breathe.

As if remembering the prize she still held captured in her hand, Shara started to move against him. Rapidly losing what little control he had left, Royce rolled her under him.

Her legs spread invitingly.

Royce lifted his head to watch her reaction as he entered her. At first her eyes widened slightly as she felt his fullness within her. Then her lids fluttered closed with a look of sheer bliss crossing her face. And then they opened again and he was drowning in deep, dusky, midnight purple.

That look alone fired a spark through him. He began to move. Deep, powerful thrusts. Her face tightened as he increased the tempo.

And then she was there.

She threw her head back, her hair a dark splash of colour against the pillow. Her mouth opened, her teeth biting delicately at her lower lip before she cried out.

And then his mind went blank as he too slipped over the edge into a spiral of sensation that racked his whole body.

'I still want to know what the A stands for,' Shara said a moment later in a wearily satisfied voice.

Royce laughed. 'Too bad. Now, you witch, unless you want me to have my wicked way with you again, I would suggest you get that gorgeous body out of bed.'

Shara looked as though she was seriously considering staying.

'Oh, no, you don't,' Royce said, wagging a finger in the air. 'We've barely been out of this bed all week.'

Shara pouted. 'Don't tell me you're getting tired of me already?'

He dropped a hard kiss on her pouting mouth. 'Not by a long shot.'

As he got out of bed Royce was struck by the notion that it would be a long, *long* time before he tired of her.

'Tell me something?' Shara asked.

They'd collapsed on the sofa following a karate session during which one thing had led to another and the Aubusson rug had got a workout of a different kind.

Royce opened one eye. 'What?'

Shara lay sprawled across his chest, her chin resting on her bent arm. 'I want to know about the woman who hurt you.'

His other eye snapped open. His body tensed in an automatic reaction he was too late to prevent.

He could tell from the slight widening of her eyes that Shara had noticed his response.

Royce deliberately made his muscles go slack. 'Why?'

Her index finger stroked over his skin. 'You know all the skeletons in my cupboard.'

Royce tapped the tip of her nose. 'Not all of them. I know you love Abba and have a secret weakness for blueberry pancakes.'

Shara groaned. 'I wish I'd never told you that. I'm going to get fat if you keep making them for me every morning.'

'Quit complaining. Our karate sessions more than work off that little indulgence.' He ran a hand down her back and over her bottom. 'Besides, I love your curves. You're what a real woman should look like—not those stick figures on the covers of magazines.'

'And was the woman you were involved with a stick figure? Or rounded like me?' she asked, proving that she wasn't about to let the subject go.

He shrugged. 'The relationship was meaningless. It's hardly worth talking about.'

'Well, I think it is.'

Royce recognised the look on Shara's face. She could be as stubborn as he was.

He sighed and closed his eyes. 'It's simple, really. It was in the early days of my career. I'd been hired by a wealthy businessman to find out which of his household staff was stealing antiques from his home. Fiona was the daughter of the house. She showed an interest in me from day one.'

Shara stole a quick kiss. 'And why wouldn't she? You're handsome and sexy and smart. Not to mention that you make terrific blueberry pancakes.'

'That earns you another kiss,' he said, putting words into action.

A long, drugging minute later he lifted his head. 'Anyway, to cut a long story short, it turned out that Fiona *was* the thief. She had a cocaine addiction she'd somehow managed to hide from everyone. She was stealing from her father to support her habit. She almost got away with it too—until I finally twigged to what was going on.'

'And how did you do that?'

He shrugged. 'I walked in one day and found her using. I added one and one together and came up with the right answer. She admitted what she'd been doing and begged me not to tell her father.'

Shara's eyes were locked unwaveringly on his face. 'And what did you say?'

'That I had no choice.'

Not only had he had a legal not to mention a moral obligation to do his duty to his client, but supporting Fiona's lies would have made him no better than she was—and that was something he just wouldn't do.

Shara was nodding her head, as if she agreed he'd made the right decision.

Royce stared at her.

Of *course* she would agree.

Her values were much the same as his.

She was as open and honest as he was.

'So what happened?' Shara asked, breaking in on his thoughts.

'That's when things turned ugly. She told me that she'd just been using me to keep tabs on my progress.'

He remembered that last scene vividly. It was imprinted on his brain.

'I'm sorry.'

He looked at her. 'Don't be. It was a long time ago. Besides, it taught me an invaluable lesson.'

She raised a brow. 'And what's that?'

'That it's better to think with your head than your heart.'

'Oh.'

Shara couldn't think of anything to say.

'You sound surprised,' Royce said, brushing a strand of hair off her face.

'I guess I am. I just…'

'You just what?'

She shrugged. 'I don't know. It just sounds kind of…cold to me.'

'Does what we share feel cold to you? Because it sure as hell doesn't to me.'

As if to prove the point, he ran his fingertips down her back to her buttocks, where they lingered for a mind-bending moment. The trail of sensation he left in his wake was anything but cold. In fact just the opposite. It felt so blisteringly hot she felt it deep inside her.

She shook her head. 'No, it doesn't feel cold.'

'Doesn't it make sense to think logically about what you're doing rather than just diving in head-first? It does to me. And I bet it does to the hundreds of divorcees who didn't take the time to realise they were totally incompatible before tying the knot.'

Shara frowned. She couldn't speak for those divorcees. She could only speak for herself.

As if reading her mind, Royce asked, 'If you hadn't been so desperate to escape your father would you have married Brady? I'm betting you wouldn't.'

Shara wanted to argue with him—she wasn't quite sure why—but she couldn't.

Looking back, there had been signs that Steve was a control freak. Once or twice there had even been hints in his behaviour that he had bullying tendencies.

Hindsight was a fine thing. She hadn't realised how she'd ignored those warning signs by simply sweeping them aside. Why?

Because at the time her father had been her most immediate problem. She'd latched on to Steve as if she was a drowning woman and he was a life-preserver. If she'd let him go...

Well, she hadn't wanted to face what would have happened—which was precisely why she'd overlooked those telltale signs that all had not been as it should and proceeded anyway.

She'd been forced to acknowledge more than once that when she was emotionally upset she almost always made the wrong decision—including the time she'd tried to slip away from Royce.

She nodded. 'You're right. It's far better to think with your head than your heart.'

The day of the court hearing arrived far too quickly. It was a dose of reality they could both have done without, but Royce was proud of the way Shara walked in, with her head held high, back ramrod-straight and chin angled challengingly. She was there to do battle and it showed.

He was prouder still as he watched her performance in the courtroom. It was exemplary. When the judge asked her a question she followed Jackson's instructions to the letter.

Keep it simple, Jackson had told her. Try and answer each question directly, without over-answering. Be calm and precise. And under no circumstances let Steve provoke you.

Afterwards Royce hugged her against his chest. 'We are going to celebrate!'

Shara looked up at him, her blue eyes wide in her face. 'We don't have to do that.'

Royce slid his hands into the small of her back. 'I know we don't, but I want to. I was so proud of the way you handled yourself in there that I was fit to burst.'

She smiled. 'Burst, huh?'

He nodded. 'It could have been ugly.'

She laughed, some of the tension in her face easing. 'I couldn't have done it without you.'

'Sure you could.'

She shook her head. 'No—seriously. Knowing you were there made all the difference. I knew I was safe with you to protect me.'

A sudden movement behind Shara caught his attention.
Brady!

A wave of anger rocked Royce on his heels—so intense that he heard a roaring sound in his ears.

A man who treated women the way Brady had treated Shara was not a man at all. He was the scum of the earth.

Royce stepped around Shara, blocking her view.

It was one thing to face Brady in the formality of the courtroom, where he was unlikely to say or do anything offensive or hurtful. It was quite another to meet him in a normal everyday setting like the corridor they were standing in, with no lawyers, judges or guards to prevent him from being his usual ugly self.

Royce hugged her to him. 'I think you're underestimating yourself.' Swinging her in the opposite direction, he grabbed her hand. 'Come on. I have just the place in mind.'

The restaurant Royce took her to overlooked Balmoral Beach. 'This place has the best seafood.'

They took their time discussing the menu. Shara finally decided on roasted Kingfish, with a beetroot, baby spinach and feta salad, while Royce chose the crisp fried whole snapper with bok choy and Asian sauce.

Since they were celebrating Royce suggested champagne. When the waiter had poured the sparkling liquid and departed Royce raised his flute. 'What shall we toast to?'

It was on the tip of her tongue to say *To us,* but that hardly sounded appropriate. It suggested something permanent—and neither of them wanted that.

Did they?

Shara was no longer so sure. Somewhere along the line she'd got in deeper than she'd intended.

Royce was a very special man. He'd helped her become the woman she was always meant to be, and he treated her as no man had ever treated her before.

As if she were a princess.

She raised her glass and stared deep into his chocolate-brown eyes. 'How about to life?'

'I like that.' Royce clinked his glass against the side of hers. 'To life.'

'To life,' Shara echoed.

'What else?'

'What do you mean what else?'

'Well, I'm feeling on a high. I think we should toast something else. In fact I think we should toast anything and everything under the sun just for the sheer heck of it.'

Shara smiled back. In this mood Royce was impossible to resist. Quickly on the back of that thought came another. Royce in *any* mood was impossible to resist.

'Well?' he prompted.

Shara drew back in her chair, hands in the air. 'Hey, don't look at me. I came up with the first toast. Now it's your turn.'

'OK. Fair enough.' He rubbed the side of his jaw thoughtfully, then raised his glass. 'To infinite possibilities!'

'Infinite, huh? There speaks an eternal optimist.' They clinked glasses again. 'To infinite possibilities.'

'OK. Your turn.'

Shara put her glass down on the table. 'I think we'd better slow down, otherwise I'm going to get drunk.'

Royce picked up her glass of chilled water, handed it to her, then picked up his own. 'Here—this should keep you sober. What's our next toast?'

Shara thought about that. *To us* was still sitting on the tip of her tongue, but it was no more appropriate now than it had been five minutes ago.

She held up her glass of water. 'To new beginnings.'

She'd expected Royce to smile. Instead he lowered his glass to the table and frowned. 'Don't think about Brady. He has no place in this celebration.'

'I wasn't thinking about Steve, I was thinking about—'

She broke off, her eyes dipping to the white linen tablecloth.

'Thinking about what?' Royce asked.

You.

For a minute she thought she'd said the word out loud. Because when she'd spoken about new beginnings she'd been thinking about him. And the new beginning she'd envisaged was of the two of them—together.

Which was quite patently ridiculous.

There were taking one day at a time. Keeping things casual.

Only the way she was feeling was anything *but* casual.

'I was thinking about the future and those infinite possibilities you were talking about,' she said, trying to force her lips into a smile. Only they weren't co-operating. 'Once this situation is over, the world is my oyster.'

The thought should have made her deliriously happy—but it didn't.

Because once the situation with Steve was over Royce would walk out of her life.

There would be no more karate sessions.

No more talks.

No more seeing him smile or hearing him laugh.

Shara swallowed—hard.

Then did it again.

Royce flashed her a megawatt-bright smile. 'Well, that's OK, then.' He raised his glass in the air. 'To new beginnings.'

They went backwards and forwards for another ten minutes, each toast becoming sillier and more outrageous.

Finally Shara flung her hands in the air and called it quits. 'You can't make a toast to blueberry pancakes!'

'Why not?'

'Because you just can't.'

Throughout lunch Royce's eyes never left hers—not even for one second, as if what she was saying was earth-shatteringly important and deserved his full attention.

He picked up her hand every so often and twined his fingers with hers. Sometimes he kissed the inside of her wrist, and the look in his eyes made her wish they were somewhere more private where she could draw his mouth down to hers.

After lunch Royce suggested a walk along the beach.

Shara looked down at her suit. 'I'm a bit too dressed up for a paddle.'

'Says who?' He grinned. 'The world is your oyster, remember?'

His grin was infectious. So much so that Shara found herself smiling back. 'So it is.'

She kicked off her court shoes, scooped them up with two fingers, and jumped on to the sand. 'Race you to the water!'

Royce beat her hands-down, but Shara didn't care, waiting patiently while he pulled off his shoes and socks and rolled up his trouser legs.

They walked the length of the beach with the water lapping at their ankles, their fingers intertwined.

They were near the end of the beach when his hand tightened uncomfortably around hers.

'Royce?' she prompted, but he wasn't looking at her. He was looking into the distance with a frown on his face. 'What is it?'

He turned back to her, the frown turning into a smile. 'Nothing. I just thought I saw…' He shook his head. 'It doesn't matter.'

Afterwards they went home and made slow, languorous love.

And as her heartbeat returned to normal Shara realised that she hadn't been this happy in a long, *long* time.

Smash!

Shara bolted upright and automatically reached out a not quite steady hand to turn on the bedside lamp and look around.

When her eyes landed on broken glass, she stared at it. Where had it come from?

And then it dawned on her—the window had been broken!

'Stay still,' Royce ordered.

He was two steps ahead of her. He was already out of bed, pulling on the low-slung jeans that always made her mouth water, and assessing the situation with narrowed eyes.

'Where are you going?' she asked as Royce headed towards the door.

'Outside. Stay there,' Royce ordered again in a hard voice. 'I'll be back in a minute.'

'I'm not going anywhere,' she said.

She watched his muscular back and tight denim-clad butt as he stormed out of the door. She could hear his heavy tread as he took the stairs two at a time before he raced through the lower level and continued outside.

Shara kneeled on the bed to take a closer look. Someone had thrown a brick through the window.

Shara shivered as she surveyed the scene. The brick had missed the bed by a matter of inches. A little bit closer and it would have hit Royce.

She paled, her insides trembling.

Swinging her legs over the edge of the bed, she used her toes to find her slippers. She rose shakily to her feet and then on wobbly legs walked to the brick and picked it up.

She weighed it in her hands, then turned it over—only to drop it again as if it had bitten her when she saw what was written on the other side.

You're dead.

She staggered back towards the bed and dropped down on to it, the crudely carved message holding her full attention.

Shara stared at the message. Her initial shock was wearing off. In its place was a deep, burning anger that burrowed inside her until it was bone-deep.

Shara welcomed the feeling. A month ago this incident would have made her feel sick and anxious. And it would have made her feel like a victim.

Now anger and frustration dominated her.

She had no doubt Steve had thrown the brick.

Who else would do such a vicious thing?

The big question was: who was the message for?

For her? For Royce? Or for both of them?

And what did it matter?

What mattered was that the situation couldn't be allowed to continue.

CHAPTER NINE

ROYCE stopped in the doorway, his face grim as he looked at Shara. His hands were bunched into fists at his sides, the knuckles showing white. Anger swelled inside him, but he forced it back.

Now was not the time to let the emotions raging inside him free rein. Right now he had to make sure Shara was OK.

Striding across the room, he sat down beside her.

'Did you see anybody outside?' she asked.

Royce stiffened. 'No. Whoever it was they're long gone.'

'It was Steve,' she said flatly.

Royce nodded, doing his best to keep his voice even as anger ratcheted up his spine. 'I suspect so.'

Shara nodded her head towards the brick. 'There's a message.'

Leaving her where she was sitting, Royce picked up the brick using a corner of the bedspread. He'd have it dusted for fingerprints but he suspected there wouldn't be any.

He turned the brick over and read the crudely carved message. Biting out an expletive, he stared at the engraved letters with an icy calm that was far worse than any level of anger could be.

It seeped through his skin and into his bones, freezing his insides to sub-zero.

This was his fault.

Fairly and squarely.

There was no one else to blame.

How many times had he told himself that emotions fuzzed your objectivity and dulled your ability to handle a situation the way it should be handled?

Yesterday he'd been so wrapped up in Shara that he hadn't even realised that Brady had followed them from the courthouse.

It had been luck, not training and experience, that had led him to that brief glimpse of the other man when they were on the way back to the car.

He'd consoled himself with the fact that nothing had happened.

But it had happened *now*.

There was no doubt in his mind that Brady had watched Shara and himself together. No doubt in his mind that it was doing so that had provoked this reaction.

Their lunch at the restaurant and their walk along the beach afterwards flashed across his mind.

No wonder he hadn't seen Brady. He hadn't been able to stop looking at Shara. The sadness he'd noticed in her eyes when he'd first met her was gone. She looked…

Well, she looked happy. And relaxed. And so beautiful that she took his breath away.

Hell, he'd been acting like a man, damn it!

A man—*not* a bodyguard.

A man moreover who had lost his emotional detachment.

A man who—

No!

He put a brake on his thoughts.

Dragged in a breath.

Reproaching himself would achieve nothing.

What he had to do now was focus. Or should he say *re*focus?

OK. So he'd got in deeper than he should have for a little while. Lost his perspective. That was no big deal.

All he had to do was take a step back. Or ten. Or however many it took to re-establish his normal objectivity.

If that meant returning to a strictly professional relationship then so be it.

Shara was the principal.

He was the bodyguard.

Full-stop.

End of story.

He glanced at Shara. 'I suggest you sleep next door in the guestroom.'

She waved a hand. 'I have to clean up this mess.'

'No. That's the last thing I want you to do. The police will want to have a look at it.'

'The police…?'

'Yes, I'm calling it in.'

'Do you think they can prove it was Steve?'

Royce shrugged. 'I don't know. I doubt he's left fingerprints. It's the early hours of the morning—the best time to make an attack because most people are asleep. If we're lucky someone saw him, or he ran a red light somewhere. But, frankly, it's a long shot.'

'Oh.'

She sounded disappointed. Royce was aware that the responsibility for that sat squarely on his shoulders too.

'Get some sleep,' he said, and walked out of the room.

Shara didn't sleep. Instead she lay staring up at the ceiling in the spare bedroom.

She heard movement in her bedroom. And voices. She wasn't sure whether it was the police or operatives from the Royce Agency.

It didn't really matter.

She'd bet money on the fact that they'd be unable to prove that Steve had anything to do with throwing the brick.

Steve wasn't stupid; he'd have covered his tracks.

Finally the house fell silent. She waited for Royce to come to bed but he didn't.

She almost went in search of him, but she didn't want to disturb him if he was busy.

Around four a.m. she fell into a fitful slumber that was filled with bad dreams. The nightmare played out like a series of snapshots.

Royce with a brick hitting his temple.

Royce with bright red blood streaming down the side of his face.

Royce lying prostrate on the floor.

Not moving.

Lifeless.

Shara could feel anxiety filling her from the toes up. As if someone had taken a jug of fear and angst and was pouring it down her throat.

Until she was completely filled to overbrimming.

Until she was choking on it.

A scream tore from her throat.

She came awake with a start, jack-knifing into a sitting position. One hand was at her chest, where her heart was jumping around like crazy, the other went protectively to the base of her throat, where she could feel her pulse racing to a similar beat.

Royce burst into the room with a force that almost took the door off its hinges. He turned on the main light and the sudden brightness made Shara blink like a startled rabbit.

He scanned the room with hard eyes. He was wearing the low-slung jeans and nothing else. His body was tensed so that each muscle stood out prominently. 'What is it? Is it Brady?'

Shara shook her head.

His eyes narrowed. 'Then what is it?'

She took a deep breath. It juddered in the back of her throat. 'I had a bad dream.'

He visibly relaxed. 'Is that all?'

She nodded, waiting for him to stride across the room and gather in his arms.

But he didn't. He stayed exactly where he was.

Shara stared at him, puzzled and more than a little bit hurt.

'Well, I'm not surprised. You received quite a shock to-night.'

'So did you,' Shara said, not able to shake the images that were seared onto her retina.

'I'm used to it. You're not.' He paused for a moment. 'Well, if that's all, I'll leave you to it.'

Shara frowned. 'Aren't you going to join me?'

He shook his head. 'I have things to do.'

'I see,' she said.

But the truth was that she didn't see. She didn't see at all. She'd heard the words. Of course she had. She'd even processed them. But they didn't make sense.

It sounded...

Well, it sounded as if Royce was making an excuse not to be with her. That 'I have things to do' had sounded like the equivalent of *I have to wash my hair* or *I have a headache*.

Maybe she was just being oversensitive—and maybe she wasn't.

Either way, she couldn't shake the feeling that something was wrong.

Royce wanted nothing more than to stride across the room and gather Shara in his arms.

When he'd heard her scream he'd frozen.

That had never happened to him before.

Normally his reaction to emergency situations was automatic. Without question.

He didn't think. He just acted. Whatever he had to do, he did it.

But this time he'd hesitated—if only for a moment.

With fear.

Not for himself, but for Shara.

Which just went to prove that he was too close. Way, *way* too close. On *every* level.

So instead of rushing across the room to hold her he forced himself to stay exactly where he was.

'Are you sure you're OK?' he asked.

She nodded. Her eyes dominated her pale face. She looked anything but OK, but he couldn't afford to comfort her.

'OK. I'll see you in the morning.'

She nodded again.

There was hurt and confusion in her eyes.

Royce hardened his heart against it.

Still, closing the door was one of the hardest things he'd ever had to do.

As soon as Royce left the room Shara rolled over and buried her head in the pillow.

Tears were pricking at the backs of her eyes but she refused to let them fall.

She didn't want to think about Royce and why he was acting so strangely. Frankly, it hurt too much—as if someone was stabbing her in the chest with a sharp knife.

Instead her mind went over the night's events, then drifted back over the past few months.

It was as if she was seeing things clearly for the first time. As if a veil had been lifted from in front of her eyes.

She'd thought she was taking her life back.

Thought she was standing up for herself.

But really she'd only been paying lip service to that goal.

There had always been someone else standing in front of her, fighting her battles for her.

She'd escaped a domineering father by turning to a man she hadn't even realised was far worse.

She'd put up with abuse that no woman should have to put up with.

And when the breaking point had come what had she done?

She'd gone running back to Daddy.

Her insides shrank in on themselves.

Since then she'd followed a path of passive resistance—until Royce had made her realise what she was doing.

Even then she hadn't really stepped up to the plate. She'd been hiding behind the law, behind Royce, behind anything she could lay her hands on.

But she was over that. Now, finally, she felt cold and determined and ready to fight. *Really* fight. She'd had enough. It was time to end this.

And one thing was clear.

If she wanted to deal with this problem once and for all then *she* needed to deal with it.

Alone.

Without assistance.

The answer wasn't going to be found in a courtroom.

Or hiding behind Royce's back.

It was going to be found inside *her*.

She had to find the guts to do what she hadn't done in the first place and stand up to Steve.

The realisation made her feel oddly calm—and oddly in control.

Her courage had been growing along with her confidence. She was ready to do this.

There had to be some way out of this mess.

But what?

Think, girl, think.

And then it came to her.

It didn't come at her like a bolt out of the blue. It was more as if another veil had been removed from her eyes.

In reality she'd known the answer for a long time. Royce had told her all she needed to know. She just hadn't been ready to listen at the time.

What she needed now was a plan that could turn the theory into reality.

Reaching out, she picked up the phone and dialled a number she remembered by heart.

Dawn was only just breaking, but he answered on the eighth ring. 'Hello?'

'Hello, Steve,' Shara replied calmly.

There was a stinging silence.

'Shara? Is that you?'

'Yes, it's me,' she said, speaking quickly, determined to show no hesitation—and no fear.

'What do you want?' he asked.

Her hand tightened around the phone. 'I just called to tell you I received your message.'

'What message?' he asked innocently.

She barked out a laugh. 'Oh, come on, Steve. Let's not pretend, shall we?'

Another silence followed. This time she sensed his surprise.

And she could understand why.

She hadn't talked to him the way she just had for a long time—if ever. She'd been too frightened of the consequences.

'I don't know what you're talking about,' Steve denied.

'Of course you do. Only little boys throw bricks through windows and then run away. Be man enough to admit what you did.'

'Don't play with me, Shara,' Steve warned. 'No doubt you and the he-man have the phone tapped and plan on trying to trap me into admitting something I didn't do. Well, it won't work. I'm too smart for you.'

For a second—just one—she wondered whether he was right.

But no.

She couldn't afford to think that way. Attitude was nine-tenths of battle. She had to walk the walk and talk the talk.

She was no longer a victim, and it was time she started acting like it.

Her hand tightened around the handpiece. 'Who's playing?'

'You are. If you think you can outsmart me you're wrong.' He paused for a moment. Even through the telephone line she could practically hear the cogs of his mind turning over. 'I'll say this much, though. This is between you and me. You had no right bringing anyone else into it. Lose lover boy.'

The implication was clear. As clear as if he'd added the words *or I'll do it for you*.

The suggestion was so ludicrous that Shara couldn't help but laugh. 'Don't even think about it. Royce would take you apart piece by piece.'

'That's what you think.'

'No. That's what I *know*. He'd make mincemeat out of you in two seconds flat. But that's beside the point.'

'Then what *is* the point? Why are you calling me?'

She dragged in a breath. 'I'm fed up with this situation. Why don't we get together and talk about it? I'm sure we can sort it out like two rational human beings.'

There was a long silence. 'What about the Restraining Order?'

'What about it? You didn't let that bother you when you delivered your message last night.' She paused for a moment, and then said. 'You're not scared, are you?'

It was a deliberate ploy. She knew Steve wouldn't be able to resist such a provocative taunt.

'Of course not,' he denied quickly. 'But if you're thinking about getting someone to photograph me with you so that you can say I broke the Restraining Order then it won't work. I'll make it clear that you invited me. And just in case you're thinking about lying then remember that the telephone records will prove that *you* called *me*—not the other way around.'

'I'm not planning on having someone take a photograph of you.'

No, she was planning something far more effective than that.

'OK. When and where?'

Shara thought rapidly, sifting through her options. She needed just the right place for the half-formed plan in her mind to work—somewhere public and open and, even more importantly, somewhere guaranteed to have a lot of people.

She wanted them visible.

'Bonito's,' she said, naming a popular café she and Steve had been to numerous times before. 'Ten o'clock for coffee and a chat.'

With that she hung up the phone. He'd be there. She knew he would. He wouldn't be able to help himself.

The sense that something was wrong between Royce and herself intensified the following morning.

As was usual, Royce was in the middle of cooking breakfast when she walked into the kitchen.

He always woke before her. He was one of those people who got up as soon as their eyes opened. Shara was the exact opposite. She liked to take her time, snoozing for a few minutes before she was ready to greet the day.

'Good morning,' she said, walking into the room.

She walked towards Royce like a homing beacon. Her intention was to wrap her arms around his waist from behind and then wait for him to turn and give her a good-morning kiss.

Royce threw her a brief smile over his shoulder, said an equally short good morning, and then turned back to the stove.

Shara stopped dead in her tracks. She stared at his back for a long moment, a sense of unease rippling down her spine.

After standing there for another minute, with not another word or look, let alone a good-morning kiss, she diverted to the fridge.

'You didn't come to bed last night,' she said, trying to keep her voice light and even.

'I slept in another room,' he said, addressing the contents of the frying pan. 'I didn't want to disturb you.'

'You wouldn't have disturbed me.'

In fact just the opposite. She'd wanted nothing more than to have him in bed with her, the hard, warm length of his body beside her, his arms wrapped around her.

'You needed the sleep.'

The hairs on the back of her neck prickled as her sense of unease deepened. She stopped part-way to the kitchen bench, a tub of yoghurt in one hand, a punnet of blueberries and a banana in the other.

'Don't tell me what I need or don't need,' she said, addressing his back.

Particularly when he had it wrong.

What she'd needed was *him*.

She almost blurted the words out loud, but she swallowed them back. Given how stand-offish and unapproachable he sounded, it was hardly the appropriate thing to say.

'You *didn't* need to get some sleep after all the fracas?' he asked, tossing the question over his shoulder.

Their eyes met. His were blank. Empty. Totally without the warmth she was used to seeing in them.

A shiver ran down her spine and her stomach shrank to the size of a pea.

'Is something wrong?' she asked, her heart beating anxiously in her chest.

She was still staring at his back intently, which meant that she saw the infinitesimal tightening of his muscles. 'No, nothing is wrong.'

But everything was wrong.

It *felt* wrong.

Royce looked and sounded different.

And she couldn't figure out why.

She wasn't imagining things.

And it hurt.

It hurt more than she cared to admit.

Royce was pretending to work—pretending because he couldn't forget the look of hurt confusion in Shara's eyes when he'd deliberately tried to blank her out—when his computer started to beep.

His head snapped up, a frown on his face.

Pulling the keyboard towards him, he tapped a few keys to take him to the household security system. The beeping indicated that the outside perimeter of the house had been breached.

One look at the monitor confirmed someone near the garage at the back of the house.

Was someone—Brady?—coming in?

Or was someone—Shara?—going out?

There was only one way to find out.

He was on his feet and racing towards the back of the house in two seconds flat.

He reached the rear door, only to find it locked. Cursing under his breath, he ran for the front door, noticed an open window and made a quick diversion. He squeezed through the opening, which he only just fitted through, and rounded the house in time to see Shara's car disappear out of the gate at the end of the driveway.

This was the first time she'd tried to give him the slip since that very first day. For a moment all he could do was stand there. He couldn't believe this was happening—not after everything that had happened between them.

'Damn it!' he hurled. 'What is the woman doing now?'

Running at full tilt, he headed for his 4WD. Shara had a head start. There was no time to lose.

He was in and had the motor running in a time that would have shamed an Olympic runner. He took off with a screech of tyres, leaving in his wake a trail of smoke and the smell of burning rubber.

As he drove his brain went to work on this latest development.

Why had Shara tried to give him the slip now?

Royce wasn't sure, but his gut instinct warned him that whatever it was it wasn't good.

Although he was already going well above the speed limit he flattened the accelerator to the floor. The 4WD surged like a hungry monster.

He raced through the streets.

His head turned left and right, searching for a glimpse of Shara's small red sedan.

He had to find her—and fast.

Shara clenched the steering wheel with sweaty hands.

She was a jumble of emotions. So much so that she could hardly string two thoughts together.

Although she was nervous about confronting Steve, her forthcoming meeting with him paled into insignificance beside what had happened this morning.

She'd been so determined not to hand over her power to a man again, and yet that was exactly what she'd done.

She hadn't seen it happening.

It had crept up on her.

And this time it was even worse.

Because this time she'd handed over the most precious thing she possessed.

Her heart.

Royce slammed on the brakes, sending the 4WD into a skidding fishtail.

Car horns blared around him. Abuse was yelled out of windows, along with a few obscene gestures. Royce ignored it all as he brought the car under control and executed a turn.

He'd just caught a glimpse of a red sedan on one of the cross streets. Although there were plenty of red sedans in Sydney, there wasn't a lot of traffic about—and it was the first car he'd seen that looked remotely like Shara's.

It was a target. The best hope he had at the moment.

Hurtling around the corner, Royce gave chase.

Shara pulled her car into a parking slot directly opposite Bonito's. She took a deep breath and looked over at the café.

Steve was already there, waiting for her.

Shara hadn't expected that. Although perhaps she should have. If Steve thought he was being set up it would be logical he'd want to reconnoitre the place. Being here before her would mean he had plenty of witnesses to say that she'd approached him, not the other way around.

Grabbing her bag, she got out of the car, locked it, and hurried across the road.

Steve was drinking what looked like a cappuccino. He didn't bother asking whether she wanted something as she sat down opposite him. He knew this wasn't a social occasion.

She wouldn't be able to swallow anything anyway. She wanted to get this over with so that she could think about Royce and what she was going to say to him when she got back to the house.

Because she had to say something.

She had to *do* something.

She couldn't just sit back and let Royce break her heart.

A lump formed in her throat. She swallowed it down and forced thoughts of Royce away.

Now was not the time.

She'd deal with Royce *after* she'd dealt with Steve.

She leaned back in her chair, as far from Steve as possible. 'So here we are.'

Steve nodded, watching her warily.

Her eyes ran over his face. In the past she'd found him so frightening. Now she didn't. Not in the same way.

Now she saw him for what he was. Not an all-powerful monster. Just a man. A bully, with a mean streak a mile wide.

Her heart started to thud uncomfortably in her chest and she took a deep breath.

It was time.

Royce frowned through the windscreen as the red sedan pulled into a parking space and the sole occupant alighted from the car.

It was Shara.

There was no doubt about it.

Although he was still too far away to make out her features, he recognised the outfit she was wearing and the magnificent fall of her hair.

She hurried across the street and took a seat at a table on the footpath outside a busy café.

His eyes narrowed on the man opposite her.

Ice slid down his spine.

His teeth clamped down tight.

It was Brady.

Royce stared—and kept on staring.

One thing was apparent.

Their meeting was no accident. It had clearly been arranged. There was no doubt about that.

Shara had deliberately and intentionally gone behind his back to meet her ex.

Betrayal bit hard and deep. So hard and deep that it left him gasping for breath.

He would not have believed Shara capable of such subterfuge.

He really wouldn't.

When he'd realised he was guilty of pigeonholing her he'd looked back on her behaviour with new eyes—and it had been quite an eye-opener.

Her reactions had appeared as if they were completely without artifice.

When he'd accused her of being a victim she hadn't hesitated to tell him that if she was a man she'd hit him into the middle of next week. And when she'd realised he was right she hadn't tried to hide her reaction. Instead she'd buried her face in her hands and called herself a fool.

The list just kept going on and on.

Her lack of embarrassment about having a meltdown and her frankness in admitting that she was tired of being scared and that she wanted more confidence.

Even the first morning she'd woken in his arms she'd been open about her feelings, telling him that she felt uncertain and anxious.

He'd been convinced that where Shara was concerned what you saw was what you got.

And yet here they were, Royce thought bitterly.

He thumped the steering wheel—hard.

Then again—even harder.

Then with considerable effort he pushed his feelings aside.

Right now he had a job to do. The fact that Shara had obviously agreed to meet Brady didn't alter the fact that having done so put her in danger.

His heart began racing. Adrenalin pumped through his

veins. Danger lurked in the air. He could smell it. He could taste it. He could touch it with his hands.

What did he do now?

He could, of course, come to a screeching halt at the kerb outside the café, jump out of the car, and snatch Shara to safety.

But he had to consider Brady's reaction.

If Brady saw him coming it could push him over the edge. Who knew what he might do?

Throwing the brick through the window had been a violent gesture. A café had knives. A bottle smashed on the edge of a table could become a lethal weapon in less than a second.

No, a stealthier approach was called for.

It would be safer.

Royce assessed the area through narrowed eyes.

There was a side street running along one side of the café. If he drove around the block neither Brady nor Shara would see him. He could sneak up on them.

The other big advantage of that plan was that Brady had his back to that particular corner. If he was careful—and he usually was—he could steal up behind Brady without the other man even realising he was there.

Swinging hard on the steering wheel, Royce made a sharp right turn and raced around the block. There were no spaces available, so he drove up a driveway and parked on the pavement in one neat manoeuvre.

He jumped out of the car even before the engine had stopped. Then, keeping close to the wall, he edged towards the corner. Once there, Royce leaned forward—just far enough to take a quick look around the end of the painted brick wall.

Brady's back was maybe ten to twelve feet from him.

Royce braced his feet against the pavement and was about to throw himself around the corner when he heard Shara speak.

'You are a pathetic loser,' she said, her voice strong and clear and cutting.

His heart lurched with shock. He froze to the spot, unable to move.

What was she *saying*? What was she *doing*?

Provoking Steve was asking for trouble.

'What did you say?' Brady's voice was low and dangerous.

'You heard me.' Shara sounded strong and self-assured. 'You are lower than a snake's belly. Just a weak little bully who gets his rocks off by pushing other people around. Well, I came here today to tell you that you don't scare me any more. You are just—'

Shara broke off at the same time as a scraping sound hit his eardrums.

Everything happened in slow motion then.

At the same time it happened so fast that it was a blur.

Royce flung himself around the corner just in time to see Brady push himself up off his chair. It fell to the ground with a loud crash that made heads turn in their direction.

Shara jumped to her feet. She didn't back away. She just stood there.

Royce was running as fast as he could, but it felt as if he was moving through an invisible glue which was dragging at him, slowing him down.

He saw Brady draw his clenched fist back in preparation for throwing a punch.

Royce was too far away to stop it happening.

'Block!' he screamed. 'Block, damn it.'

But his instruction wasn't needed. Shara was already moving into action, her body jack-knifing straight, her left arm shooting upwards to block the punch that was already halfway to her face.

She blocked.

And then she punched.

Brady staggered backwards before crashing to the ground.

Several patrons jumped to their feet. A waiter arrived, demanding to know what was going on.

Royce ignored all of it.

He grabbed the tops of Shara's arms. 'Are you all right?'

She nodded, shaking her hand in the air. 'I think so. Although my wrist hurts.'

Royce swung on Brady, who was rising to his feet. 'Down,' he commanded, as if he was ordering a dog to sit. 'Or, as God is my witness, I will punch you so hard you won't ever get up again.'

Brady subsided back to the ground.

Royce glared at the waiter. 'Call the police.' Then he gave a general stare around the café. 'Don't any of you leave. You're witnesses to what happened here.'

The police arrived. Asked questions. Took statements.

Royce wanted to wrap his arms around Shara and hold her close, but the knowledge that he'd crossed a line he'd promised himself he'd never cross stopped him. Instead he contented himself with standing at her side the entire time.

Finally it was over. Brady was taken away in handcuffs.

Royce led Shara to his 4WD. After seeing her inside, he rounded the bonnet and got in beside her.

What had just happened—what had almost happened—flashed across his mind.

He saw again the fist directed towards Shara's face. It if had connected it could have broken her nose or her eye socket or worse.

Worse still was seeing his reaction with the benefit of hindsight.

He'd frozen—again.

Which just went to prove that taking a step back and re-establishing their professional relationship had been the right thing to do.

So why, then, was there an ache in his chest that threatened to consume him?

CHAPTER TEN

SHARA glanced at Royce for the hundredth time since they'd got into his 4WD.

He hadn't spoken a word since they'd driven away. His profile looked as if it had been cut from the hardest and most unyielding granite. His hands were gripping the steering wheel so tightly that his knuckles had turned white. The atmosphere was so thick you could cut it with a knife.

They were halfway home before Shara got up the nerve to break the silence. 'Well? Aren't you going to say something?'

His hands clenched and unclenched around the steering wheel. 'Not while I'm driving.'

His words were clipped and abrupt.

'I know you're angry, but—'

He spared her the briefest of glances. 'I'm not angry. I'm beyond anger. But I would rather postpone our conversation until we get back to the house.'

Shara fell silent, a deep frown creasing her brow. She glanced at Royce again from beneath the shield of her lashes.

Royce wasn't lying. He wasn't angry. He was…

Cold. Emotionless. Distant.

Even though he was sitting right beside her, he might as well be sitting a million miles away.

Her insides turned to ice. She wrapped her arms around herself.

As soon as they were inside the house Royce turned to her. His arms were folded in front of his chest, his face grim. 'I thought I'd seen an end to this nonsense, but I should have known better. What on earth possessed you to sneak out of the house like that? How dare you go behind my back and meet Brady?'

Royce hadn't spoken to her this way for a long time. Not since those first few days when they'd clashed over her need for a bodyguard.

Stalling for time, she asked, 'How did you know I'd gone anyway?'

'I connected my laptop to the in-house security system the day I arrived and I've been monitoring it ever since. But that is beside the point. Why on earth did you agree to meet Brady? And why on earth didn't you tell me he'd contacted you?'

She remained silent.

Royce was speaking to her like a bodyguard.

Not like her lover.

This conversation underlined the radical shift their relationship had undergone since last night.

Why he'd changed, she didn't know.

The important thing was that he had.

'Shara?'

She dragged in a breath, trying to ignore the pain in her chest which she knew was the feel of her heart breaking into a million pieces.

She angled her chin into the air. 'I arranged the meeting.'

She heard the air rush from his lungs.

'Are you *mad*?' Royce roared.

'Don't yell at me!' Shara ordered.

She was proud of her reaction. Not that long ago if anyone—particularly a man—had shouted at her she would immediately have shrunk in on herself.

Now she had the guts to counterpunch—just as she'd had the guts to punch Steve in the face.

Royce dragged in a breath, then said calmly, 'I repeat. Are you mad?'

'No. I'm not mad. I just decided it was time to end this once and for all.'

As she spoke Shara realised that the decision to end this once and for all didn't just apply to Steve.

It also applied to Royce.

It had to.

She'd asked Royce if anything was wrong and he'd said no.

Once she would have sat back and let him get away with his behaviour. She'd have let him go on hurting her.

Now her self-preservation instincts were much stronger.

She was much stronger.

Even though it was going to be the most difficult thing she'd ever had to do she had to cut Royce out of her life before he hurt her any more than he already had.

And she knew just how to do it.

'By getting yourself killed?' Royce demanded, breaking in on her thoughts.

'You're exaggerating.' She waved a hand in his direction. 'You trained me yourself. The odds were on my side. At the worst he might have knocked me out or given me a black eye. But that's a small price to pay for my freedom, don't you think?'

Royce stared at her, his eyes so wide they were deep, dark pools. 'Let me get this straight. Are you saying you *planned* this? Are you saying you intended for him to hit you?'

She nodded.

Royce's big body jerked as if he were a marionette and an invisible hand had just yanked on his strings. 'What on earth would make you do something so stupid?'

'It wasn't stupid,' she said defensively. 'It makes perfect sense.'

'And just how do you figure that?'

'You said it yourself.'

He frowned. 'Said what?'

'You said, and I quote, "If Brady crosses the line once the AVO is in place we can have him arrested."'

'I didn't mean for you to set yourself up,' he said sharply.

'I know you didn't. So don't go beating yourself up over it. I made the decision because I'm tired of this entire situation. I wanted—no, I *needed* it to be over so that I could get on with my life.'

Royce stared at Shara.

Why did he have the feeling that she was talking about more than just the situation with Brady?

Why did he have the feeling that she was talking about *him*?

'What are you saying?' he asked.

He waited for her to smile. Make some kind of light remark about the world being her oyster or something similar.

But she didn't.

In fact there was something about her expression that wound his stomach into a tight ball.

Something was wrong.

He knew it. He could *feel* it.

His gut instincts were finely tuned and usually accurate.

The eyes that met his were ice-blue, with not a skerrick of warmth in them. 'I'm saying that it's over. Finished.'

His stomach muscles tightened some more. 'What is?'

She waved a hand through the air. 'Everything. Including us. I've come to my senses, you see.'

Her voice was cold. Her eyes even colder.

Royce frowned. 'What do you mean you've come to your senses? About what?'

'About what's been going on here.'

His eyes narrowed at her tone. 'And what exactly *has* been going on here?'

'You've taken advantage of me.'

Royce reared back as if she'd slapped him. 'I've *what*?' he bit out incredulously.

'You took advantage of me,' she replied in that same calm tone. 'Your job was to protect me, not seduce me. Is this how you get your kicks? Seducing frightened women into sleeping with you?'

'No. It is not.' He walked further into the room. His movements were stiff, uncoordinated. 'I do *not* make a habit of sleeping with clients. The way you're talking anyone would think I forced you to sleep with me, and we both know that's not true. You were more than a willing participant.'

She nodded. 'You're right. I was. If you want to know the truth I confused gratitude with desire.'

Royce stiffened. The length of his spine contracted, vertebra by vertebra. 'Explain,' he snapped out.

She shrugged. 'You made me feel safe for the first time in a long time.'

He heard the words. Of course he did. He wasn't deaf. But for several long seconds they made no sense to him.

And then they did.

They ripped through his psyche like a bulldozer ripping up concrete.

His hands clenched into fists at his sides. 'Are you saying that you slept with me out of *gratitude*?'

She nodded. 'That's exactly what I'm saying.'

Memories flashed into his head.

The day he'd rescued her from Brady Shara had flung herself at him and said, 'Boy, am I glad to see you!'

Just the other day after the court hearing Shara had said, 'I knew I was safe with you to protect me.'

Hell, she was right.

Why hadn't he seen it before?

His chest felt tight, as if a heavy weight was crushing it.

He opened his mouth to say something—he wasn't sure what—but just as quickly shut it again.

What was the point?

Their relationship was over. He'd already decided that. Her betrayal in going behind his back had merely nailed that decision solid.

It no longer mattered why she'd slept with him—except it did.

It mattered one hell of a lot.

Royce clenched his hands into fists. Dragged in a breath.

All he wanted to do was grab her and demand some answers. But that would be a mistake—because he would be allowing his emotions to make decisions for him.

If ever there was a time to apply cool, calm logic to a situation it was now.

'Fine,' Royce clipped out, making a slashing movement with his hands. 'I won't bother you again.'

She seemed to pale, but surely that was his imagination.

'You most certainly won't,' she said, using her best hoity-toity tone. 'You won't get the chance.'

Royce raised a brow.

'Steve is in jail, therefore your services are no longer required.'

Royce frowned. No matter how unpalatable and distasteful he found the conversation, and her accusations, there was no way he was going to leave her unprotected. 'That may only be temporary. He could be out on bail within twenty-four hours.'

She shrugged, looking completely unconcerned. 'That doesn't matter. Don't you see? Standing up to him the way I did today set me free. I'll never be scared of him again. And he knows it.'

Royce searched her face. Her inner strength shone as brightly as her outward beauty. 'You mean that, don't you?'

She nodded. 'I do. That's why I had to meet him alone. I had as much to prove to myself as I had to prove to Steve. If it's any consolation, you've helped me reach this point.'

It was no consolation at all. Although it proved that Shara had had a damned good reason for going behind his back—an acceptable reason, even—he still felt as if a big, dark thundercloud was hanging above his head.

'I'll fight to keep him in jail,' Shara continued. 'I don't want any other woman to have to go through what I've gone through. But Steve no longer has the power to hurt me.'

Royce stared at her.

He couldn't argue with her rationale.

Like most bullies, Brady had targeted Shara because she was unlikely to retaliate. After her performance today he would know that was no longer the case.

Shara was right.

There was no reason for him to stay.

Which should have been cause for celebration.

Why, then, did it feel as if she'd just shot him through the centre of his chest? As if the life force of his blood was gushing from his body and draining away?

His spine lengthened until he was standing as tall as it was possible for him to stand. Every muscle in his body was as stiff as a board.

He wanted to rant and rave. He wanted to demand that she take back every word. He wanted to tell her that he was staying and that was that. End of story.

But none of that made any sense.

So he simply said, 'Fine,' for the second time in as many minutes.

For a split second he thought he saw a shadow of pain flit across the surface of her eyes, but he decided he was mistaken.

Without saying another word he spun on his heel and stalked out of the room.

He didn't say goodbye.

He couldn't.

Royce didn't remember walking into the lounge room and zipping his laptop into its case. He didn't remember walking up the stairs and packing his belongings. He didn't remember getting in his car and driving away.

He was operating on automatic pilot.

He didn't want to think. Or feel.

It wasn't until a car horn blasted behind him that he came back to reality.

He stared at the traffic light and registered that it was green. From the continuing blare behind him it obviously had been for some time.

He pressed his foot down on the accelerator. The car surged forward.

He drove for about a hundred metres before he slammed on his brakes. The action earned him another horn blast, this time accompanied by a couple of expletives.

Royce rested his head on the steering wheel. His heart was racing, his breathing short and shallow.

It felt as if he'd sprinted that last one hundred metres.

His lungs felt fit to burst.

He felt fit to burst.

He thumped a clenched fist on the steering wheel and then did it again.

This was all wrong. Wrong on so many fronts he could hardly count them.

He'd thought this was what he'd wanted, but it wasn't.

Driving away from Shara had made him realise that this was not what he wanted at all.

He'd spent so much time thinking and analysing and rationalising and trying to be his usual cool, logical and reasonable self that he hadn't even realised he'd been fooling himself.

Slamming the car into gear, Royce spun it around. Then, pressing his foot to the floor, he hurtled back in the opposite direction.

Shara sank down in the middle of the Aubusson rug, trailing her fingers over the fine weave.

Tears were close, but she refused to let them fall.

This was where she'd fallen in love with Royce.

Right here in this very room.

She could see him now, in the black loose-fitting cotton pants and singlet he'd always worn during their karate lessons. She could see his smile and the lock of hair that fell across his forehead.

She could hear him saying, 'Again!' in that determined voice of his as he pushed her to do her best.

He'd given her so much—probably without even realising he was doing it.

And how had she repaid him?

By letting him walk away without telling him the truth.

Worse, by telling him a bunch of lies that reduced what they'd shared to a travesty.

Her fingers stilled on the carpet. Her body grew rigid. Her eyes widened.

She pressed a hand to her chest, her mind whirling with thoughts.

'My God, I've done it again,' she whispered out loud. 'How could I be such a fool?'

Once again she hadn't taken the time to think things through.

She'd been hurt.

So hurt that she'd lashed out without thinking.

She should know by now that making decisions in the heat of the moment always backfired on her. When she was emotionally upset she almost always made the wrong decision.

Why hadn't she remembered that?

She thought back to the conversation they'd had on the roadside. It felt like eons ago.

Royce had accused her of playing the victim, of choosing a course of passive resistance where Steve was concerned.

And wasn't she doing the same thing now, with Royce?

Royce had taught her to fight back—so why wasn't she fighting now? Fighting for the man she loved instead of showing him the door?

She should have stamped her foot, or used one of his own manoeuvres against him and forced him to tell her what was wrong. She should have used every piece of ammunition she possessed to fight for her man.

She'd found the courage to confront Steve. Now she needed the courage to tell Royce exactly how she felt about him.

Shara scrambled to her feet.

Then she raced for the stairs, snatched up her car keys and headed for the garage.

Royce swung hard on the steering wheel and with a screech of tyres fishtailed into the Atwood Hall driveway.

His eyes widened, the breath locking tight in his lungs as Shara's small red sedan loomed in front of him.

She was travelling at a rate of knots—practically hurtling down the driveway.

Reacting automatically, he slammed on the brakes and swung hard on the steering wheel, trying to avoid a collision.

He briefly registered the look of panic on Shara's face before she did the same thing.

The only problem was she'd swung her car in the same direction as his.

Royce cursed and pressed even harder on the brake, even though it was impossible to depress it any further.

Thankfully their quick thinking worked.

When the two cars came together it was with the kiss of

bumper bars. Royce didn't need to look to know that there
would barely be a dent.

He sat where he was for a count of ten, waiting for his
heart to slow.

Then he pushed the door open and got out.

'Are you mad?' he roared. 'Are you trying to get yourself
killed for the second time today?'

Shara slammed her hands down on her hips. 'Don't yell at
me.'

Her eyes were a fiery blue but Royce didn't mind. Anything
was better than the way she'd looked at him earlier. As if he
wasn't there. As if she was looking straight through him.

'I'll yell at you whenever you deserve it. Where on earth
were you going at a thousand miles an hour?'

She lifted her hands off her hips and jammed them down
again. 'Excuse me? *You* were driving like a maniac. You almost hit me.'

'But I didn't.'

'What are you doing here anyway?'

Royce folded his arms in front of his chest and stared her
straight in the eye. 'I came back to call you a liar.'

She blinked. 'What did you say?'

'I said you're a liar,' Royce replied calmly.

'And just how do you figure that?'

Royce dragged in a breath.

Images from the last few weeks flashed across his brain.

Shara laughing.

Shara teasing him.

Shara staring up at him with eyes like stars as his body
thrust into hers.

He took a step towards her and then another. 'You did *not*
sleep with me out of gratitude.'

She didn't answer him. She just stared at him with deep,
fathomless eyes.

He took another step towards her, clasped the tops of her

arms. 'Simple gratitude would not make you look at me as if you want to eat me alive. Simple gratitude would not make you cry out my name or dig your nails into my back when I made love to you. I may make you feel safe, but I also make you feel a hell of a lot more than that.'

To prove it Royce swept her into his arms, right there in the driveway.

He kissed her as if there were no yesterday and no tomorrow. As if this moment in time was all that existed.

When they were both breathing heavily, Royce lifted his head and put her away from him.

Shara's lashes flickered open. She stared at him with desire-drenched eyes. This was the soft, wonderful woman he was used to seeing.

'Now look me in the eye and tell me why you lied,' he said softly.

Shara blinked and blinked again. The daze of desire slowly faded from her face. Something flickered in her eyes, and then the air whooshed from his lungs as she punched him forcefully in the chest.

His wide eyes fixed on her face.

Had he thought she was soft and wonderful?

Huh!

Try strong and angry!

'What did you do that for?' he demanded.

'Because you deserved it.' She shook her hand in the air. 'That hurt.'

'Serves you right.' He took her hand in his and gently massaged it. 'You're going to make me regret teaching you karate if you're going to start picking fights with everyone.'

Shara angled her chin into the air. 'Steve deserved it, and so do you.'

'What makes you say that?'

'You know why, damn it! You rejected me.'

He *had* rejected her. And by doing so he had hurt her. He'd caught a brief glimpse of her pain but he hadn't wanted to acknowledge it.

Because acknowledging it meant confronting what was inside him.

Leaving her had made him confront it anyway.

'I know I did. I'm sorry.'

She didn't look the least bit appeased. 'Why? Did I do something wrong?'

He smudged his thumb across her lower lip. 'You didn't do anything. It was me.'

'I don't understand.'

He sighed. 'I know you don't.'

'Well, you're not leaving here until you explain it to me,' she said, thrusting her hands on to her hips. 'So start talking!'

Royce stared at her for a moment, and then he flung his head back and laughed.

Shara really was a changed woman.

His chest swelled with pride...and something else.

'I realised that when I was around you I was acting like a man—*not* a bodyguard. Doing so could have put you in danger.' She opened her mouth to speak, but before she could Royce continued. Shara had proved that she was the bravest woman he'd ever met. He had to prove that he was her equal by doing the same thing. 'At least that's what I told myself.'

Her eyes narrowed in on him. 'So if you weren't worried about putting me in danger, what made you back off the way you did?'

'Can't you guess?'

Shara stared at him for a long moment, then shook her head.

Royce dragged in a breath. He'd faced some dangerous situations in his time. Even life-threatening ones. He'd dealt with each and every one of them with courage and daring.

And yet telling Shara how he felt was almost enough to

bring him to his knees. 'I was losing my emotional detachment. You more than anyone know how vulnerable that can make you feel.'

He heard her sharp inhalation of breath. Saw her eyes widen. 'You mean you—?'

Royce ran a finger down her cheek. 'Yes. I mean I love you.'

'You do?' She frowned. 'But if you love me why did you push me away?'

'Because I was scared.'

'You? Scared?' She sounded incredulous—as if it were impossible that he could feel that way.

'Yes, me.'

'But you're not scared any more?'

'No, I'm not. Driving away from you was the hardest thing I've ever had to do. I just couldn't do it. I had to come back.'

She stared him straight in the eye. 'Do you know where I was going when we almost collided?'

Royce shook his head, his heart doing a stutter-step when he realised how close he'd come to hitting her. 'No. I just hope it wasn't another hare-brained scheme of yours.'

'It wasn't hare-brained,' she protested.

'You're not safe to be let out on your own,' Royce continued, as if she hadn't spoken. 'You need me around to keep you out of trouble.'

'I agree.'

'I mean it. You—' He slammed his mouth closed. 'What did you say?'

'I said I agree.'

'You do?'

She nodded. 'I do. In fact I think I might need a permanent bodyguard.'

His heart thumped. He glanced at their cars, which were still sitting nose to nose, then turned back to Shara. 'Where *were* you going?'

She stared at him. Her magnificent blue eyes were filled with an emotion that made his heart beat even harder. 'I was coming to find you.'

'You were?'

She nodded. 'I was. Do you want to know why?'

His heart stopped thumping and made a massive leap into the back of his throat. 'Yes.'

'Because I decided I'd made a mistake. I sent you away because you'd hurt me, but watching you leave was even more painful. You taught me to stand up and fight, so I was coming to find you—to fight for my man.'

His heart swelled until it was fit to burst. 'Do you mean it?'

Her eyes met his. 'Yes, I mean it.'

Royce stopped breathing. So many thoughts and feelings rushed through him that he didn't know which way was up.

Not sure what to say, not sure what to feel, he pulled her into his arms and crushed her mouth with his.

By the time he lifted his head they were both breathing heavily. 'Are you sure?'

She nodded.

'Say it,' he demanded.

She didn't question what he meant. She obviously knew he wanted to hear her say the words.

'I love you,' she murmured softly.

And it was there in her face.

It had been there for him to see, only he'd been too blind to see it.

The glow in her face. Her eyes gazing at him like stars.

Royce closed his eyes and savoured the words, felt them filling his bloodstream. He opened his eyes and stared down at her.

'You *have* to tell me now,' she said breathlessly.

He frowned down at her, taking in the mischievous gleam in her eyes. 'Tell you what?'

'What the A stands for.'

He laughed. 'Do I have to?'

Shara nodded. 'If you love me, you have to tell me.'

'That's blackmail.'

'Quit stalling.'

'Aristotle,' Royce muttered.

Shara wrinkled her nose at him. 'Awful.'

He nodded. 'Awful. Promise you won't ask me to give any of our children such an awful name.'

Her expression changed. 'Children? You want to have children with me?'

'I certainly do,' he said firmly. 'Although I want you to myself for a while first. Let's wait until we've been married for a couple of years before starting a family.'

'Married…?'

That was it. That was all she said.

He cupped the side of her face. 'Maybe I shouldn't have mentioned it yet. It's probably too soon. I know you had a bad time with Brady, so I can understand if you're a little hesitant about getting married again. But I want to put my ring on your finger. I want the world to know you're mine. So think about it.'

'I don't have to think about it.'

Her expression was so serious that his heart dropped to the pit of his stomach and then kept right on going. 'But—'

She laid a finger across his lips. 'No buts.'

'But—'

'Let me finish.'

Royce snapped his mouth closed. She could finish—but he wasn't taking no for an answer. Defeat was not a word in his vocabulary.

Shara smiled. 'You're not very good at following instructions.'

'What are you talking about?'

Her eyes twinkled. 'If you want my co-operation what do you need to do?'

His face cleared. Then he dropped on one bended knee. 'Shara Atwood, would you do me the honour of becoming my wife?'

Her eyes misted. 'Why?'

'Because I love you with all of my heart.'

Shara flung herself at him. 'Of course I'll marry you. Just try and stop me.'

His lungs seized, then started working again. He let out a whoop that could probably be heard throughout the entire neighbourhood and then swooped, taking her mouth with his.

* * * * *

MODERN™

INTERNATIONAL AFFAIRS, SEDUCTION & PASSION GUARANTEED

My wish list for next month's titles...

In stores from 16th December 2011:

❏ The Man Who Risked It All — Michelle Reid

❏ The End of her Innocence — Sara Craven

❏ Secrets of Castillo del Arco — Trish Morey

❏ Untouched by His Diamonds — Lucy Ellis

In stores from 6th January 2012:

❏ The Sheikh's Undoing — Sharon Kendrick

❏ The Talk of Hollywood — Carole Mortimer

❏ Hajar's Hidden Legacy — Maisey Yates

❏ The Secret Sinclair — Cathy Williams

❏ Say It with Diamonds — Lucy King

Available at WHSmith, Tesco, Asda, Eason, Amazon and Apple

Have Your Say

You've just finished your book.
So what did you think?

We'd love to hear your thoughts on our 'Have your say' online panel
www.millsandboon.co.uk/haveyoursay

- 🌹 Easy to use
- 🌹 Short questionnaire
- 🌹 Chance to win Mills & Boon® goodies

Visit us Online

Tell us what you thought of this book now at
www.millsandboon.co.uk/haveyoursay

Special Offers

Every month we put together collections and longer reads written by your favourite authors.

Here are some of next month's highlights— and don't miss our fabulous discount online!

On sale 16th December   On sale 16th December   On sale 6th January

Save 20%
on all Special Releases

Find out more at
www.millsandboon.co.uk/specialreleases

Visit us Online

0112/ST/MB353